PACHA'S PAJAMAS
A Story Written by Nature

by
Aaron Ableman and Dave Room

*"There can be no keener revelation of a society's soul
than the way in which it treats its children."*
—Nelson Mandela

Pacha's Pajamas: A Story Written By Nature,
Third Edition / Children's Novel

Printing History: First Edition - 2011 (AARON ABLEMAN)
Second Edition – 2012 (AARON ABLEMAN)

For information please contact
BALANCE EDUTAINMENT.
5807 Fremont Street
Oakland, California 94608
(510) 285-7075
www.pachaspajamas.com
www.balanceedutainment.com
ISBN: 9781613643556

Contact for media or publishing inquiries:
info@pachaspajamas.com

Praise for Pacha's Pajamas

"*Pacha's Pajamas* is the children's book series we've all been waiting for—a gift for teachers, parents, and anyone who engages with young people. Aaron Ableman and his all-star team have crafted a heartfelt, inspirational story with unforgettable characters and imagery. Reading the first book, *Pacha's Pajamas: A Story Written By Nature,* reignited my imagination!" ~Meena Srinivasan, author of *Teach, Breathe, Learn: Mindfulness In and Out of the Classroom*

"*Pacha's Pajamas* will open the minds and hearts of countless children, introducing them to the magic of Mother Nature in her wondrous manifestations as plants, stones, animals — all of her resplendent forms. This book is a blessing. A must 'read and share' with all you know." ~ Michael Bernard Beckwith, bestselling author

"*Pacha's Pajamas* is a fun, creative and beautiful way to engage children in helping reconnect with the Earth and all of the life that we share our home with. To inspire and re-inspire all people—of all ages—to care for the Earth, each other and all life is vital for our human species to not only survive, but to thrive. And creativity like *Pacha's Pajamas* plays an important role in this, our collective story, and our work." ~ Julia Butterfly Hill, renowned author

"A big thumbs up! Pacha's PJ's includes so many wonderful themes for children and adults. It takes the reader through the experience of being with all the animals and how elaborate they are described and how realistic they come to life. It is a great start to really help kids become aware of very important issues in our times and to get them off the couch and out into nature." ~Academic's Choice Awards

"This story about a little girl's dream—where all species unite to support a healthy planet—will play a catalytic role in building our movements for change. Please invite everyone you know to buy this book!" ~ Van Jones, Author/TV Personality

"A beautiful story for both children and adults to help us all visualize the world that can be." ~ David Korten, author, *The Great Turning and Agenda for a New Economy*

"*Pacha's Pajamas* is an eloquently written and timely fable that will not only inspire children AND adults to DREAM of a healthier, more sustainable planet, but also inspire them to TAKE ACTION!" ~ Joel Harper, author, acclaimed children's book, *All the Way to the Ocean*

"I'm a fan of education that's practical and that is fun, and not just in the classroom. And this project has applications across the board! A good thing about something like *Pacha's Pajamas* is it's spreading important information early, so it becomes like a cornerstone or a foundation." ~Talib Kweli, Renowned Artist

"From start to finish, *Pacha's Pajamas* is an amazing musical story. A Story Written By Nature is sure to be a hit and inspire kids everywhere! *Pacha's Pajamas* delivers!" ~ Indie Music Digest

"I love *Pacha's Pajamas* because of the empowering message it gives children about their future and the environment. The story speaks to their need for an environmental hero, and they quickly saw themselves in her. As a pediatrician, I understand the accumulating scientific evidence that kids must get outdoors and into nature for their health. How to get them there is always the dilemma. Artists and entertainers are invaluable partners in the healer's quest to engage kids in the natural world." ~ Nooshin Razani, Mother, Pediatrician

Acknowledgements:

Giving thanks for the Great Spirit of life, that which is beyond name or number. Deep gratitude to the indigenous spirit inside ALL OF US, singing in ancestral voices that remind us to love ourselves, our relatives and the planet upon which we depend. Massive appreciations to the Ableman family, the Williams family, the Room family, the Jonson family, the Marin family and all of the family ethic that has stood behind this project! Nuff' respect for our global community of dreamers – from the awesome collaborators to the studio engineers' to the fire circle of musical storytellers – calling forth a masterpiece from the heart. Big gratitude the editors Steve Barancik and Lorna Apper for their devotion to the craft, Andrew McGovern of Zahada.com for helping design Mr. Ticks map, Erika Minkowsky, Zanette Johnson and Elisabeth Garst for their angelic support. So much love to all of our Kickstarter backers! Give thanks for all the kids, musicians and artists involved in this legacy project. Immense gratitude to the luminaries and authors who have written testimonials including Seena B. Frost, Meena Srinivasan, Rev. Michael Bernard Beckwith, Vandana Shiva. Julia Butterfly Hill, Mona Polacca, Mos Def, Van Jones, David Korten, Talib Kweli, and Joel Harper. Our deep gratitude to Armin Wolf & Christine Schoefer, John Smith & Family, Phil Jensen, Jaime Moore, Joseph Muratore, Warren Strudwick, Robin Room, Leila Monroe, Erik Olson, Greg Jensen, Rafe Eric Biggs, Ritu Agarwal, Ras Carey, Bobby Cortes & Family, Maureen Shea, Magik Santos & Family, David Christopher, Kent Lewandowski, Chris McDavid, Walter Jackson, Suzanne Toro, @ak2webd3, Teresa Lopes, Richard Naylor, Victor Douglas, Bud Smith, and Leslie Smith for believing in this vision. Big thanks to our advisors including Ralph Guggenheim, Yu-Kai Chou, Elana Yonah, Amelía Aeon Karris, Mr. Williams, Karen Robert Jackson, Arne Jin An Wong, Jimmy Cummings, Jessie Vukoson, Micheal Leifer, Ahmed Rahim,

Bryant Terry, Carter Collins, Kate Liegey, Philip Zimbardo, Rosa Gonzalez, Rue Mapp, Zero Nylin, Rose Yee, Aaron Lehmer, Zero Nylin, and Ras Carey.And infinite praises to Rev. Elouise Oliver, Rev. Dereca Blackmon and the EBCRS community, Rev. Michael Bernard Beckwith and the Agape International Spiritual Center, Allah El Henson, Melia, Mari, Avalon Theisen & Family, Dawna Shuman, Lynn Hasselberger, Elle Perrault, Nooshin Razani, Mathieu Senard, Jyoti, Salina Espinoza, Avery Cleary, Jackie & Michael Carlyle, Diane Johnson, Peregrine Zoe Whitehurst, Joe Mohr, Jessa Hurley, Lucas Guilkey, Dayna Regerro, James Palombo, Dulce Juarez, Tracy Pan, Kay Cuajanco, Shamini Dhana, Colin Miller, Robin Milam, Gerardo Marin, Ernesto Olmos, Ambessa Cantave, Leif Wold, Lynne Elizabeth, Drew Dellinger, Brian Stross, Stephanie Lipow, Alex Hill, Kevin Connelly, Lois Bridges, Katrina Hammer, Karen & Winnie Poon, James Nixon, Umi Says, Mark Stafford, Angela & Fleurette Sevin, EZ Yonah, Marisa Murgatroyd, Debbie Harlow, Ryland Engleheart, Raj Ramaya, Luke Archer, Kat Steele, JoAnna Claassen-Luttner, Nicole Solis, John Griffith, Peter Luvaas, Nancy Nadel, Susan Silber, Monifa Bandale, Lev Laltoo & Family, i.am.mani, Shani Wade, Yonatan Landau, Jeff Shiu, Pancho Ramos Stierle, Verenice & Sol, Ricardo Gressel, Kat Thompson, Ama Zenya, Sita Davis, Ayse Gursoz, Annie Leonard, Marc Finser, Diana Cohn, Bud Smith, Rich Saleh, Brigitte Griswold, Nimo Patel, Nipun Mehta, Jonny Kloberdance, Ras K'Dee, Rahul Iyer, Raphael Jesus Gonzales and everyone in the "Despierta" crew. Big thanks for all the organizational support and inspiration from Youth Leader, Dhana, Inc., Aurasma, Earth Guardians, Children & Nature Network, Pachamama Alliance, Mindful Life Project, Homeless Prenatal Project, Social Venture Network, B Lab, AppBackr, 13 Indigenous Grandmothers Council, Cafe Gratitude, Global Exchange, Global Alliance for Nature's Rights, Alter Eco, Service Space, Karma Kitchen, Karma Tube, O'Melveny & Myers, Amphibian Survival Network, Green For All, Destiny Arts Center, Ankh Marketing, Impact Hub Bay Area, and Impact Hub Oakland!

Table of Contents

Prologue 1

Little Girl, Big Dreams 3

Trouble in the Waters 10

Mr. Tick 18

The Mask 24

The Big Idea 29

The Spirit of the Earth 34

Tell the World 40

Greatness is Hard Work 48

Welcome to Pacha Jamma! 55

Message in a Bottle 63

Lay of the Land 70

Monkey Traps 78

The Storm 86

Stop, Rock and Roll! 101

Use What You Got 107

The Final Dance 113

Who I Really Am 120

Epilogue 127

Fun Facts 131

Afterword 136

Prologue

Sitting under the only tree in her school playground, Pacha daydreamed about meeting a platypus at the edge of a river. The platypus told her that no matter who you are, you must "use what you got" to bring your dreams to life. He said his dream was to keep the rivers cool... he didn't want his family to be fried platypi! And he also taught her the Duck Dance!

Interrupted from her daydream by the bell, Pacha made the mistake of running into her science class yelling that the rivers and oceans are heating dangerously, the polar ice caps are melting, and "what will everyone do without ice cream?!" She was immediately teased for being a crazy "Nature Girl" and the bully in her class made her never want to say anything again in public. Yet, something inside her had awakened, a force of nature beyond words.

1

Little Girl, Big Dreams

Pacha was a little girl with big dreams. Her dreams were bigger than the biggest elephant at the zoo. Her dreams were bigger than the Andes Mountains, homeland to her parents and ancestors. She dreamed of lost secrets and upside-down rainbows. She dreamed of dancing in front of huge crowds. But her biggest dream was to be an everyday hero, like discovering the cure to sadness or conquering sickness with a deep breath.

Sadly, real life wasn't so dreamy. Pacha was feeling a little fluster coming on. Maybe it was the weird weather lately and the storm clouds rolling through her city (though they really could use some rain). Maybe it was the tinge of smoke in the air or that she had to dodge trash blowing through the streets. That AND she had to perform the next day in her school's Earth Day musical! Whatever

Pacha's problems were, life sometimes seemed easier when she hid in her room or at the zoo caves, frozen in time like a frog under a winter lake.

When Pacha and her father arrived home from school, she started wheezing and coughing.

"I can't breathe! I...feel like...Ms. Wheezer blew a hurricane down my throat!"

It was another terrible breathing attack and her toes scrunched up in pain. Ms. Wheezer was a name that she had given her breathing problem, trying to make

it sound as silly as she could so that it wouldn't be so serious. But that didn't work this time, as this felt like the worst attack ever.

With blue lips, she huffed and puffed. Her father calmed her by cuddling her into his arms, encouraging her to let the feelings pass like clouds in the sky. She finally found her breath as she took a deep draw on the inhaler er father held for her. As if right on time, her mother entered the front door.

Pacha's mother set the groceries on the floor. "Amor, did you have another attack?"

Pacha fell into her mother's arms and cried: "But why does this happen to me?!"

Her Mother responded calmly, "Ai mi vida, I know this is so hard for you, but let's remember that struggling only makes it worse. If you see life like a dream, even night-mares can't take you off track!"

Pacha was still sobbing though: "Can you ask Ms. Wheezer to get a new job? I'm sick of being sick!" She cried again, still feeling a choke in the back of her throat.

"Well, you're the only one that can fire Ms. Wheezer...but I have something that could help ... something for you to wear like a hero's cape, especially on nights like tonight."

With that, Pacha's mother brought out a colorful pair of pajamas, which looked like they were glowing. They were covered with dancing animals and singing plants. "These are magical pajamas!" her mother said lovingly. "When I was your age, my mother made me a pair of pajamas woven from baby Alpaca — a fabric once used by royalty and medicine people. She told me that every woven stitch was a prayer, thanking Pachamama for my life."

"¡Ai, Mamá! They're as soft as a chinchilla's belly!" exclaimed Pacha as she giggled for the first time all day. Hugging her mother and feeling a tingle of hope in her heart, Pacha closed her eyes. She imagined the PJs were a new best friend or a magic carpet carrying her to distant lands or a wingsuit to fly with hummingbirds. Perhaps this pair of jammies could be her new dream-catcher? Somehow being around the pajamas made her remember all of the things she loved about being a kid.

That evening, as Pacha put on her new PJs, she had a funny feeling that her life was changing. What's more, she had lots of questions for her father.

"Does the sky breathe?" she wondered, curious as to whether the sky noticed all the smoke and storms in the air these days. "And, before people, did animals make the rules?"

Pacha paused as her eyes rested on an old gorilla mask on the shelf near her bed; it was still hanging around from the Halloween performance last year when she forgot her lines. Putting it on, she pretended to dance like a goofy gorilla, exclaiming, "Can I be a dancing *girl-illa* in these pajamas?" as if all her problems had gone away.

Her father laughed and said, "So many questions, mi angelita. Maybe if you jump in bed faster than a little cheetah, you will find the answers in your dreams."

Pacha stuffed the gorilla mask into her pajama pocket, snuggled into bed and drifted off into a dream.

2

Trouble in the Waters

It all began when a whale shouted to a hummingbird — something that doesn't happen in just any dream. From the ocean to the forest, the enormous grey whale called out to the wee bird.

"Help! Help! I'm drowning!" yelled the whale.

The crimson-chested hummingbird stopped mid-air, and hovered above the wild splashing beneath her at the ocean's edge. Pacha, who was hiding behind a tree near the shore, stood shocked by what she was seeing, as if she was in a scary movie. When the whale cried again, Pacha felt a choke in her own throat! "I wish I could help that whale but I can barely breathe myself," she thought. Pacha swallowed a tear as she watched the bird zip down to the whale's side.

The whale's deep voice gasped, "Something is stuck in my blowhole!"

Pacha wheezed into a fold of her PJs, which comforted her nose like a silk handkerchief. She wanted to help the whale, but felt nauseous and helpless.

Pacha focused back on the action in the water, amazed that the animals were speaking in her language. The only animals she'd ever heard talk were beatboxing parrots and singing goats in funny videos. Pacha squinted as the tiny hummingbird peered into the hole on top of the whale's head. Using her tiny beak and all of her strength, the colorful bird pulled out what looked like a bag from a grocery store.

The slow-speaking whale took a deep breath, spouted and said, "Thank you for saving my life! You never know how nice it is to breathe until you can't. Have my kind lived for over 50 million years just to wash up to shore with the sea trash? But please, let me introduce myself... my name is Wilder The Whale, the baritone-bass in the Seven Sea whale choir!"

"You're most welcome Wilder. My friends call me Hum. I'd say you're one lucky whale. I have always loved whales. I never knew little ole me might help someone as big as you. If only someone were filming, we might have gone viral!"

Pacha chuckled at Wilder's response, "Or maybe we could create our own reality show called *Awesomest Animal Rescues*?"

Pacha smirked, watching as Hum zipped above a tree branch above her and overlooking the sea.

"It's true, I've never seen this planet so bad in my whole life! Birds everywhere are fighting over scraps of garbage! Just the other day, an albatross friend of mine discovered an island of trash floating in the ocean and said it looked bigger than Los Angeles! What's happening?"

Hum started to cry little hummingbird tears.

"It's no wonder there are so many angry birds!" Whale sputtered.

To which Hum responded, "I can't figure it out! Even the bees of the PolliNation are disappearing by the millions... what do we do?"

Pacha hid behind a tree, wondering if she should join the troubled animals or stay out of sight for a bit longer. She wanted to help, but didn't want to startle them or do anything awkward like the time she interrupted her entire class to blab about a platypus and the world ice-cream supply. It was a good thing she hid too, because out of nowhere, a jaguar appeared in a suit and tie. The jaguar looked awfully sad and had tufts of hair missing from his body.

"Jag, what's wrong? You look terrible!" said the Hum.

The burly cat sniffed the wind, raised his golden eyes to the sky and cleared his throat. "The planet is angry and so am I! I've been running along the edge of the rainforest for hours without so much as a drop of water all day. Every time I stopped for a drink I was chased off ..."

Pacha finished his sentence in her mind, "by humans?"

Before finishing the thought, however, the big cat continued. "But let me not forget, I bring news from the Organization of Organized Organisms. There is a war... between the hungry and hungry for more. The jungle is shrinking day by day and something in the air is making the weather act strange. If things keep going this way, I may lose my job!" The upset feline rose on his hind legs and ripped off his tie. "Time, like the rain that fills our watering holes, is running out."

Pacha wanted to join the animals, but she worried that as a human they might blame her for their problems. Plus, when she spoke up in groups, she often sounded like a squeaky mouse in a crowd of elephants. So, rather than introduce herself at that moment, she climbed the tree, and watched silently as she stood on a branch.

Just then, Pebble cracked out from a boulder in the grass and shouted; "Ya'll think you have it bad? There's a crack in my heart and it's fracturing more everyday! My friends are being blown up and ripped away from their underground families. They're traded, used and then thrown away ... and I can't do anything about it because I'm just another sandstone fighting to keep myself together! We can't just keep waiting around, watching the world fall apart ...

Like an old haunted house, Tree creaked into the conversation, "I have problems too, but mine are worse than an

upset spider monkey on a bad hair day!"

When Pacha realized that she was sitting in a talking tree, she choked like her tongue dropped into her stomach. She would have jumped down, but that would have revealed her to the animals, which she wasn't ready to do. But the tired old tree continued:

"All we trees do is give, give, give...and we get so little in return! I feel like Giving Tree times a thousand. I just hope that I don't turn into another dead stump like so many of my aunts and uncles. Whatever happened to a simple *Thank You*? This year is supposedly the year of the forest, but maybe they should rename it the year of the saw."

15

A terrifying shiver went through the tree, shaking Pacha to her core. Pacha looked around to get her bearings, in case she needed to jump. When she looked down, she saw that the old toy gorilla mask had fallen out of her pocket and onto the ground.

When Jag growled "My kind has had tough relations with humans for millennia," Pacha figured that it might not be the best time to introduce herself.

Pacha looked around for a quick way to recover the mask lest the animals look for its source. She was overcome by danger below and stormy clouds above. She felt out of breath again, and wanted to reach into her pocket for her inhaler but knew that it would make too much noise. At times like these, Pacha really just longed for her parents. If Mama were here, she'd flip Pacha's frown upside down. And if Papa were here, he'd say something that would help Pacha see her way out of the situation.

Just as Pacha felt like she would blow her top, a mushroom popped up from the earth and asked, "Why is everybody so down in the dumps? All things can change, and I can change ANYTHING! I am Señor Champignon and I can turn plastic into guacamole! I can change trash into compost to feed the gardens and help the forests regrow!"

With that, another stray gust of wind blew down through Tree's branches, nearly knocking Pacha from her perch. As the wind blew, she was struck in the shoulder by one of Tree's limbs. At first she thought it was just the gust of wind, but then it crossed her mind that the Tree might really be attacking her. Maybe the Tree didn't like a primate in pajamas? Pacha tried her best to avoid the branches swaying about her but they only grew more violent. Just as she was stepping to another branch, her pajamas snagged, and she lost her footing...

3

Mr. Tick

In the grasses down below, Mr. Tick was having a bad day too. As he crawled back to the stage he wondered, of all times, why a "fire drill" had to happen on his big moment of glory, the Parasite Summit. How could it be that just when everyone got outside to the grass, a huge gorilla face fell from the sky, causing everyone to act like Chicken Littles? Much to Mr. Tick's frustration, the mask was now blocking several of the entrances to the outdoor theater, making it tough to get back to their lawn-chair seating. But seeing that everyone was more or less getting back together, Mr. Tick grabbed a microphone, apologized for the disruption, and launched into his story.

"When I was just a young tick, I thought I wanted to be a bed bug and live off the crumbs of humans eating breakfast in bed. In my teens, I wanted to be a cockroach, and eat the crumbs on the kitchen counter–more variety. In my adulthood, I worked to spread my fame like a virus. But now that I'm older, I am happy to be a simple tick." He huffed and puffed with his sagging belly, "We ticks, like good parasites, bypass human food and go straight for the jugular!"

The crowd erupted in a scary chant, "Juggalo! Juggalo! Juggalo!"

Mr. Tick talked like a smarty-pants and always yelled to get his point across. "Parasites! We know we have done great with the rise of domesticated humans! But with the help of other species who also live better with humans, we can keep this gravy-train going forever!"

"We are also lucky to have in our very presence, some high-level ambassadors from the rodent kingdom. They are thinking about my proposal for a truce between us and to strike a deal between all species that live better with humans. Thank you again for being here," Mr. Tick exclaimed as he pointed out three elderly blind mice in dark overcoats and sunglasses near the front. He huffed and puffed again, "Do you have any messages that you would like to impart from the great order of Rodentia?"

One of the mice hopped onto her lounge chair and said, "We bring greetings and good tidings on behalf of mice, rats, squirrels, guinea pigs and hamsters everywhere. We, like you parasites, thrive in human cities and live much fatter in or near human homes than in the wild. The outback just isn't as good as In-N-Out burger, if you know what I mean. As a result, we are all excited to hear

and see what you are proposing, especially for the name of this new group. Thank you!"

Mr. Tick, who hadn't yet thought of a good name for the new group of species who love humans, waited for the crowd to die down. "With the participation of our rodent friends, we will then be able to bring onboard the dogs and cats, which will seal the deal! With your support, we will keep human population growing just like it is today." His fat belly rubbed against the microphone, making a grumbling sound for everyone to hear.

"And why do we need your support? Because there is more food for us than ever before! Seven billion humans and counting is more than we ever imagined. This is a good thing not only for parasites, but for rodents and all species who live off of the strange yet powerful two-legged. If we keep things going, small will be the new big!"

Roars of ticks, rodents, wasps, louse, bedbugs and fleas echoed across the grassy knoll, where they licked their lips. To show its agreement, a tapeworm yelled out:

"You make a great point, Mr. Tick. We parasitic worms love the new varieties of human available these days! The large human tastes like bacon, the little human tastes like candy. My favorite flavor is french fries; I can smell them a mile away!"

But Mr. Tick wasn't done yet: "That's right! Just imagine eating as much as you like, whenever you like, whatever you like, with whomever you like. Doooo whaaaatya like! Freedom is knowing where your next meal is coming from ... forever! Working together on the basis of our common relationship with humans, we can create a New Food Order! As the human footprint grows, so shall we!"

The crowd chanted, "NFO! NFO! NFO!"

Mr. Tick then picked up two baby plants and raised them over his head. "Today we shall plant two special plants to remember this day; the new kings of the plant kingdom! They fatten up more people than any others. And the best thing is they are set to take over the gene pool. Yes, parasites and rodents, I am talking about genetically modified corn and soybeans. These engineered plants are what will make our dreams come true!"

But just as he said that, he heard a gasp from above, looked up to see a human slipping from a tree branch, and - as if in slow-motion - falling towards him. Like that, Pacha crashed directly on top of Mr. Tick, scattering the entire event into chaos.

4

The Mask

The drama continued all around Pacha as she collected herself from the fall. Luckily, she landed on the leaf litter - and Mr. Tick's map - which seemed like padding on the forest floor. Her fall stung but not as much as she would have expected. Plus, she was determined not to let a moment of clumsiness give her away to the wild beasts.

Hum, however, heard Pacha hit the ground and swooped down to see what had happened. Hum looked shocked and concerned. But when Pacha looked up at Hum with tears in her eyes, it was like a daughter to her mother. The bird whispered:

"Are you ok, nena? Don't worry, it's a good thing you fell off the backside of Tree – I think Tree was too busy worrying to notice that you aren't her average climber!

I'm the only one who knows of your arrival. And as long as you quickly put your mask on, you'll be alright ... everyone knows gorillas often hang out in trees."

The gorilla mask was smiling at Pacha from a couple feet away. Pacha grabbed the mask, strapped it on, and with Hum's help, nudged the mask perfectly in place.

Pacha smiled about her new disguise. It was then that she felt a prick on her hand! She looked down and saw a bug trying to burrow into her thumb! When Pacha saw the critter, she squealed like a pig on its way to a barbecue. In fact, she squealed so loud that she startled the fat bug from finishing his chomp. The bug screeched and yelled from the side of his mouth, "What are you doing you crazy faker! You can't stop the one and only, Mr. Tick!"

But Hum chimed in. "Stop you?! If you ever try to harm her again, I'll spear you with my beak and eat you for dinner!" The bird shocked Mr. Tick so thoroughly that he went cross-eyed with anger.

Still, Mr. Tick eased up on his attack, complaining, "But if you really knew the truth, she just ruined my entire life... the very least I can do is ruin hers!"

Pacha reflected on the events she was experiencing. A slow talking whale? A nervous hummingbird? An angry jaguar? And now a rude tick with an English accent?

To Mr. Tick, Pacha had ruined everything, so he spat a rhyme at her:

"Fee-fi-fo-fum,
I smell the blood of a human one,
As she lives, until she's dead
She'll rue the day she saw my head."

There was some severe questioning from Jag and Pebble, who were suspect of a lil' gorilla in pajamas. Pacha held her breath, terrified that she would be discovered as the large cat sniffed her down. But the pajamas must have smelled like a funky gorilla, because Jag backed-off immediately.

Pacha was very relieved. Hum mused, "Anyway, nothing seems natural about nature these days."

Señor Champignon suggested there were more important things to do than question a little gorilla in pajamas! While the rest of the group shifted their attention to Señor, Hum hovered over Pacha. The little gorilla hadn't said a word, for fear that her human accent would be caught by Jag or the tired old tree, who didn't seem to like humans. Much less humans pretending to be animals!

Hum and Pacha, with an upset Mr. Tick on her shoulder, joined the conversation. The whole group formed a circle around Tree, trying to get to know each other. The whale was learning birdcalls with Hum. Tree was speaking mushroom and Pebble was learning to roar with Jag. Pacha and Mr. Tick were having a fierce staring contest.

Señor proposed they talk about changing the world. Pebble asked boldly, "What about everyone who doesn't want to change?"

Mr. Tick added, "What about the ones who like the way things are going?"

Señor bounced around and said, "I am going to answer your questions with a question. Listen up, Lil Gorilla. What did the teacher say to the vegan hot dog vendor?

The others didn't have a clue. Señor continued, "The teacher said, 'Make me one with everything!'"

The group laughed. Thankful for a moment of silliness, Pacha giggled, imagining a mushroom ordering a vegan hot dog. Señor continued, "The hot dog vendor gave him the hot dog with everything on it but didn't give him his change. The teacher asked, 'Wait, where's my change?' to which the hot dog vendor said, 'Change comes from within!'"

The creatures chuckled and smirked. Pacha was amused but feeling out of breath and a little sick to her tummy. Maybe that's what the mushroom meant by changing from within? Pacha said, "But ... but ...Señor... you said, *All things can change!* What does that even mean?"

This question seemed to excite the mushroom and he lit up like a firefly. "It means...all things come and go, like clouds en el cielo de la via!"

"But what does that have to do with me or any of us here?" asked Pacha confused.

"It means...we need to look at the bigger picture! We need to do something together... something really, really special — bigger than when my cousin Myco performed for the entire Mycelial network. How can we change ourselves and not change the world? Real change comes in many ways, from the inside or the outside, from good times or from challenges ... but everything changes when we start working together!"

5

The Big Idea

But Mr. Tick loved being an arrogant pest, "Well...if you want to change the world, you're going to have to fight for it!"

The strange-colored mushroom was quicker than the speed-of-thought, "Are you a pest looking for a pestilence? Can't you see that Wilder is catching his breath, Hum is jumpy, Jag is angry, Pebble is heartbroken, and Tree is worried sick? Not to mention, the gorilla in pajamas looks like it swallowed a frog! Anyway, we don't need anymore fighting! We already have enough problemas!"

At that, the entire group erupted like a volcano:

"I am concerned about the family tree; we are the lungs of the earth!" said Tree, moving with the wind.

"We need to clean up the oceans and the rivers. Water is the blood of the planet," spouted Wilder.

"Why can't we protect our climate? Let's keep Pachamama happy. Our livelihoods depend on it!" said Jag, stroking his furry chin.

"Let's keep the tops on mountains and the oil in the soil!" said Pebble.

"I think we need more things to eat at the buffet line!" said Mr. Tick, speaking out of the side of his mouth again.

Pacha coughed and choked, feeling dizzy.

"I think we need to change the diapers of the world..." said Señor Champignon, winking at the sky

Hum zipped around the entire group. "We need overcome our selfish ways," she said looking skittishly at Mr. Tick. She quickly turned towards the others, "We also need to learn to listen to one another."

But they were all talking at once, so no one heard what anyone else was saying. To Pacha, it sounded like a bad movie blaring in another language. She began to sob. Her breath grew worse and she began to pant for air. Finally, when she couldn't take it anymore, she screamed out:

"AAACK! Help! Help!"

All of others stopped talking at once and turned to the Lil Gorilla. Concerned, they rushed to her side and

comforted her. Hum flapped some fresh air toward her, creating a natural inhaler, "Relax Nena, we are all here for you." After a few moments of sweaty palms, Pacha began to breathe easier.

Señor Champignon was the first to speak, "Ay caramba! Life is too precious to choke on it...even if the situation smells like rotten eggs with old mustard – it's really just time to make compost!"

Disgusted, Mr. Tick yelled, "I think that when you have a problem, just fight your way out of it! Life sucks, like a bad party with straws and no drinks, but the secret to winning the war is by getting started!"

The mushroom responded by jumping almost a foot off the ground, as if struck by a lightning bolt. He turned the colors of the rainbow and announced, "I totally disagree! I think that a party might be an answer for this changing world! Of course, changing the diapers of the world will require us to work together, but can you think of a better way to work together than having a party?"

The creatures looked at each other curiously. Nobody argued that they didn't like a good party. The Lil Gorilla was first to smile, then the wee bird, followed by Pebble, Whale, and Tree. Some even laughed as the Lil Gorilla lightly hummed a pop song.

Señor Champignon kept going, "Growing up in the barrios, between two concrete slabs I had to learn how to be a fun guy! I found out that if you want to change the world, you have to throw a better party!"

The group bounced with excitement. Pebble and Mushroom spun in place. Hum zipped around Tree who took deep breaths and swayed in the breeze. Jag and the Lil Gorilla roared like crazy. Everyone smiled with their beaks, fangs, or whatever else they had to smile with. Everyone except Mr. Tick, of course, who was upset that Señor Champignon had flipped his party idea.

Cracking his back and stretching, the Pebble asked, "Can you help me understand the larger message you're saying here, Señor Champignon? I'm sorry, but sometimes I'm a little dense."

The mushroom responded, "I share all of these ideas with you because I've learned that even when we're scared, sick and don't know how to change, we can always do something to make life a little better for everyone."

The mushroom popped up again and shouted so loud that even the sleepy whale jumped with a splash.

"I think we need to throw a Nature Festival!"

6

The Spirit of the Earth

The creatures had mixed feelings about the idea. Pebble was weighing the option heavily. The Little Gorilla and Hum were interested in how to create something out of nothing. Jag and Tree seemed worried about whether this would be just another festival where everybody forgets why they even come. Mr. Tick was actually "ticked-off" by the crazy idea and ready to organize a world war instead.

Just then, Pacha noticed that something else had caught Mr. Tick's attention stirring in the grass. It was a mob of parasites and wasps that had avoided Pacha's catastrophic fall. They were eavesdropping and watching everything that was happening.

"I wonder what they are doing here," swallowed Pacha, imagining ticks on lounge chairs at the beach sucking on people's necks with long straws. Pacha then noticed Mr. Tick giving the parasites a secret wink.

"What in the world is a Nature Festival?" asked Tree, still confused by the mushroom's crazy idea.

"A Nature Festival is a concert for all species to sing and dance together! It's also a place for plants and animals to share and enjoy the miracle of music, art and conversations about how to heal our mother earth... It might be our last chance to unite the world and create a better future!" exclaimed Señor.

Hum whizzed around, aflutter with excitement. "Could the eagle and the condor have a duet?"

Just then a platypus washed up from the edge of the forest, where a river flowed into the ocean. He looked familiar to Pacha but she couldn't remember from where. He splashed his head up and said: "If you guys are having a big party, can I perform one of my soon-to-be hit songs?"

But Tree responded gloomily, "I don't know about all of this! It could be a disaster trying to get billions of crazy creatures together. What if the pine beetles eat all of the trees? Plus, the mosquitoes will bother everyone! And what if a hurricane comes? I don't think I can go through with this. Unless we can create some very real ways to solve problems, it's just going to be another stupid party."

Mushroom offered:

"Maybe, instead of having just one big party, we could also have different stages or groups focused on delivering their message! We could have a stage for each biome. We'd have a stage in a swamp or a marsh, a coral reef and a river or an estuary. We'd have a farm stage. We'd have stages in savannahs, temperate forests and grasslands, the jungle, tundra, the ocean and a desert."

The mushroom continued. "And I know the perfect place where all these biomes come together. That's where our festival could be. That way we can all come together for the main show, and species that share a biome home or face the same problems, can figure out what the heck they are going to do to turn things around! We draw them in with music and dancing on the Main Stage, and then put ourselves to work on solving their problems with their neighbors on the biome stages."

"Sounds like a gigantic amount of work, even to me," said Whale slowly with a huge spouting sigh.

But the rough and tough Pebble leered at the huge whale and the mighty tree, "Why are you two scared of standing up for something you believe in or diving deep for what you love? I'm with Señor Champignon on this. Everything CAN change! I was once a huge boulder, now I'm just a small stone. Someday, I'll be sand! Together, we can move mountains. It may be hard, but I'm ready to rock, y'all!"

The wise jaguar cleared his throat and howled. "Long ago, when I was but a cub, my mama told me that where I come from, the spirit of nature, is known as Pachamama.

Long ago, Pachamama was connected to all of her children and life was in balance. But now, she is quite sick. Pachamama is calling to us!"

Jag's story awakened long-forgotten memories and stories from Pacha's childhood. She imagined her brightly dressed abuelita, cradling her while singing stories about Pachamama. She recalled her mother telling her that she was named after Mother Earth. She remembered how when she used to play in the dirt and jump in mud puddles her father would call her "Pachamamasita."

The memories shook Pacha to her core. Chills moved from the earth through Pacha's feet and legs arriving in her heart. She realized if Pachamama is Mother Earth, then Pacha means Earth. She remained curious, knowing there was probably more to these old stories.

The stately feline continued "And we can't have the trees worrying about pine beetles, hummingbirds worrying about hawks, or gorillas worrying about ticks. We must do something never done before – we need to stop fighting and eating one another. We need peace! I suggest that we call a worldwide truce for the entire nature festival – from soup to nuts!"

Mushroom seconded the motion and Mushroom called for "Ayes". Everyone agreed except Mr. Tick who abstained with his fingers crossed behind his back because the First Rule of Parasites is "don't kill your host."

As she was listening to the fallout from Mr. Tick's comment, Pacha noticed a tiny spider gliding down from the tree.

The other creatures fell silent as the spider cleared her throat to speak to the group, "My name is Eve. I have heard you speaking of an earth party to reconnect the world wide web of life. If so, I'd like to give it a spin. This won't be so easy, but it does seem like an idea whose time has come!"

Pacha focused on the spider's web, which oddly looked like the planet earth from space. The entire group watched hypnotized while Eve wove the continents into the earth web. She showed how the earth was out of balance, strangled and sick of being sick. But the spider continued speaking. "Close your eyes to see! Breathe in to breathe out. Whatever problems you have or you see in your life, let them go for now! Be a warrior for peace, not a worrier! The only thing that endures is change!"

As difficult as it was, and for first time all day, everyone started to relax. Pacha got a tingly feeling in her body. With a spellbinding speech, Eve explained that the nature festival was in fact a quest for nature itself to go to the next level of awareness – action, and that the Lil Gorilla would have a special role to play!

The magical spider then guided the group in breathing together and in imagining what it would be like for the spirit of the earth to be healthy again.

Her rivers, lakes and oceans clean.
Her forests green and tall.
Her air pure, fresh and pristine.
Her whole universe treated with love and awe.

At that moment, as if the planet had heard their prayers, the earth shook, fire from a volcano exploded into the sea and a rainbow appeared across the sky!

The Lil Gorilla jumped up and said, "It's a message for us! How about we call the festival PACHA JAMMA in honor of Pachamama, the spirit of the earth!"

The rest of the group agreed. "Let's do this!"

7

Tell the World

But as Pacha soon found out, it's a lot easier to talk about doing something than to actually do it. Especially when no one had ever done anything like the biggest festival ever. Naming the event "PACHA JAMMA" seemed like the only thing they all could agree on. There was so much to do and yet everyone had different ideas of what should be done.

Jag wanted famous leaders and presidents to speak about the climate. Pebble wanted rock & roll music. Señor imagined connecting all the networks, so all species could share stories and photos. Wilder wanted the festival to be broadcast to all water areas worldwide, following the flow of natural water cycles. Hum hoped the Main Stage would highlight the "endangered species" to make sure their gifts wouldn't be lost forever. Tree wanted extra attention on sharing ideas about what to do with the problems of the world. The little platypus just wanted to sing and rap ... and sing and rap and sing and rap forever!

But Pacha noticed that every time they almost agreed on an idea, Mr. Tick would start an argument about why it was stupid or boring. At first she thought she could just plough her way through the bickering, like how she resolved the issue of where they would have the stages. She simply stomped her feet and drew some dusty lines across the ground with her big toe:

"Let's just have the stages divided by natural borders – like where the polar tundra meets the forests or where the tropics meets the desert – so that everyone can have their special area and not keep fighting about things that don't matter to them!"

"I love it!"chimed in Señor. "These natural areas are like habitats and each of them can have a stage to host "teams" who solve the problems of the world. It'll be like that crazy insect festival called Burning Mantis ... but without all the loco's!"

Still though, they needed someone to be in charge of these stages. Someone needed to make sure everything was running smooth and on time with the sun or moon clocks. This was obviously a difficult job, especially with all the big goals of the festival.

Pacha was feeling a little itchy and concerned under her gorilla mask. She realized that if everyone didn't have a role to play, they'd all keep stepping on each other's toes. This whole idea about who should be in charge of the "Action Stages" was no different. Nobody wanted to do it! Well, nobody wanted to do it, except for Mr. Tick, who seemed eager to be in charge wherever he wasn't wanted.

"This festival is missing something that I can help with … There are lots of starving creatures that would love to come and make merriment. Like, for example, my parasite brothers. No one has even thought of them! Maybe we pair each of them with a mammal for food, travelling or dancing on? I say all of this because if we don't make things right for the parasites, we'll surely have a mutiny! And I wouldn't want to see a species war destroy your little love fest because of a simple error…"

Jag clenched his jaw and shook his head in bewilderment. Hum's chest puffed up angrily and Tree bristled her leaves in annoyance. The cool platypus ducked under water in fear. Pacha was frustrated by these crazy threats from an insect who looked uglier than an earwig after a sleepless night.

"Any…way…" said Pacha, rolling her eyes and trying to avoid a fight. "Can we talk about how we're getting the word out about this festival? We have a giant event to produce not a paradise for parasites."

Pacha wasn't exactly volunteering though. She didn't really want to chase a bunch of crazy animals to a party nor did she want to be in charge of these Action Stages either! She worried that she might bumble her words or forget her message from the stage. In addition, part of her worried that if anyone found out she was a human, they might feed her to the crocodiles. She thought the "truce" might not apply to humans.

Since no one really wanted to be in charge of the Action Stages, they decided to focus on getting the word out about the festival. Thankfully, most of the others were excited to get the word out about PACHA JAMMA to their "families" even though they knew it would be difficult, if not dangerous.

Though the Lil Gorilla was not thrilled about "getting the word out" either – she felt handicapped by her lack of experience in the wild – she wanted to do her part anyway. She was asked to tell all the primates, of course. She just hoped that she wouldn't mess up her first solo mission. Unfortunately, her worries came true the night before leaving, coughing and sneezing like an allergy in a hay field.

Before resting under a tree for the night, she told Señor that she wasn't sure if she should be the one to send the message out to the primates. Señor responded, "Don't worry...we're all kind of like the moon; we have our shadow sides... but don't let what you can't see spook you or stop you. Being a hero is about being scared and doing it anyway!"

Moving through the temporary setback, the Lil Gorilla was uplifted when Señor thanked her for being so valiant and facing her fears.

The next morning, before they left, everyone agreed on some basic rules. First off, leave no trace. Short cuts are ok, if no one gets hurt. Species-ism is not cool. Honesty is mandatory. In the final huddle before they left, they each put a hand, paw, flipper, wing, or branch together in a circle. Looking each other in the eyes, everyone shouted together in unison "Go Team!" and zoomed off in different directions like a snow flurry.

Pacha watched as Pebble rocked and rolled the news to the mountaintops and down to the valleys. Tree branched out and gave invitations far and wide, even working with her apple friends to send tree-mails through the farms. Hum spread the word to all of the flowers. Whale made a million calls with her beautiful ocean songs. Mushroom had fun telling the fungi. The spiders spun instant messages across the real World Wide Web. MC Plat sang his watery way throughout the rivers and fluvial paths. Finally, after spitting on her PJs with frustration, Mr. Tick jumped off Pacha's shoulder, scurrying off into the forest like a parasitic bandit. She was thrilled to get rid of that annoying bug, at least for a little while.

Pacha took a deep breath. With PACHA JAMMA tree leaflets in a satchel across her chest, she started down a trail. Though she knew she had to reach all the continents to tell the primate world, she had no idea how to get there. Still, she hoped to reach at least 10 monkey meteorologists, 9 bonobo builders, 8 orangutan engineers, 7 tarsier scientists, 6 lemur librarians, 5 bushbaby bankers, 4 marmoset midwives, 3 ape architects, 2 gorilla gardeners and one handy howler.

Pacha felt she had set out on the next leg of an epic adventure. At first, she thought she could skip across the whole world! But skipping got old really soon. And walking felt like she was a tortoise in deep sand. Recalling how quickly the others zoomed off, she felt discouraged, knowing that she might be walking for months like a gypsy with no caravan. "Why Me?!" she asked herself.

A voice responded, "Would you like a ride?" The Lil Gorilla looked over to see a beautiful black horse. The Lil Gorilla smiled and hopped on thankfully. The horse's name was Buster, a friendly stallion. Buster explained how he had trotted off from his home at the stables when a gate was accidently left open. A week had passed and Buster was having a hard time being free. "Once you get out, what does one do? I don't know where my family is, and all my friends are still racing or jumping. I've heard that there are wild horses and great things in the world to see, but I would love someone to experience it with!"

The Lil Gorilla said, "Well, it just so happens that I need to invite primates all across the world to a nature festival that will bring all of the species together as one. Let's boogie!"

Pacha felt the horse pick up the pace. As her excitement grew, Pacha noticed that the more she trusted Buster, the more Buster trusted Pacha. Soon, they were in perfect harmony and it seemed as though Buster knew where to go naturally. "A friendship based on trust can make miracles!" yelled the wise horse. Soon, they were moving at warp speed, even passing trains and sports cars. As the racehorse galloped from urban jungles to vast and

dense forests, the Lil Gorilla gave PACHA JAMMA invitations to the leaders, presidents, kings and queens of every primate nation. All in all, she told 543 species, 72 genera, and 16 different families!

8

Greatness is Hard Work

Back at the festival location, things were more challenging than she could have imagined. When the others saw the Lil Gorilla, they were relieved and happy to hear that so many primates had been invited. Primates are, after all, some of the loudest, most violent, and tough to work with. The Lil Gorilla and Buster shared the best stories around the fire, including how they eluded some poachers in the Congo.

The next morning, Jag rose on his hind legs to open the meeting, "Thank you all for your dedication to getting the word out! It looks like it's working, as we've heard from thousands of species around the world that they're coming to the party!" He continued, "There's just a few things to work out. First of all, who is going to be in charge of these Action Stages we talked about. I think each of you could be a great Action Stage Leader." Jag, stroked his beard, and looked into the eyes of each of the organizers, except for Mr. Tick. Jag continued, "I propose that we have a secret vote to see who gets the job." He chuckled as he handed out voting cards. Each of the others, including Pacha, wrote a short story about why they wouldn't be good for the job, except Mr. Tick who seemed to think the job was a cakewalk.

Nevertheless, when all cards were counted, every vote except one was for the Lil Gorilla. Pacha didn't understand why she would have been chosen even though she had so little experience and didn't like speaking in groups. She hesitantly accepted the role of Action Stage Leader, which also involved several short speeches on the Stadium Stage about what was happening on the Action Stages. Everyone, except for Mr. you-know-who, applauded the Lil Gorilla for her bravery and willingness to take on this important job.

"If I don't do it, I'll be like another one of those primates who only thinks of themselves while the world is crying and dying for help...your problem is my problem I guess."

Changing the subject finally, Jag roared that they still needed to figure out who would perform on the Main Stage, besides the typical rock rock-stars. Wilder spouted and said that ALL SPECIES should get at least 15 seconds of fame and that performances could be in any style. Hum zipped about excitedly, suggesting they go 24 hours a day, so that the nocturnal creatures would feel welcome too. Señor Champignon popped-up with another great idea, saying that the whole festival should be about CHANGE! Everyone loved that idea, except for the genetically modified corn and soybeans that had recently taken root in the area. They had already changed enough.

Peering through a hollowed out pair of carrot-binoculars, Pacha could see that the festival grounds were actually connecting all the different biomes of the world. From the tropics to the mountainous snow to the ocean blue, every climate and species could survive in this diverse wonderland. Already, she saw campers arriving, mainly

bugs marching into the insect quarters or camels carrying things. The fleas were setting up a market for exchanging supplies and selling food.

Hum held a contest to design the stadium and many teams submitted ideas. The marine mammals and the amphibians wanted the stadium to be an enormous underground crystal cave. The cats wanted it to be shaped like a giant milk bowl. The Tree suggested they skip the risky stadium idea and just put the performances in a redwood grove. But an osprey, assisted

by a magpie and robin had the winning design –
a ginormous BIRD'S NEST!

Looking at the plans, the Lil Gorilla and Hum once again
realized how large a project this really was. In the wind,
they sent word for volunteers to help with the building.
Pebble gathered huge dump-loads of sand and got the
bedrock for the foundation to the stadium. Tree and all
of her cousins donated massive branches. Mushroom
helped everyone find a task and gave "pep talks"
whenever they got tired. When a Spider put the word out
for master builders, the ants, termites, birds, beavers and
other spiders arrived to support.

Millions of species helped ship and deliver the equipment
for the stadium. The lightning bugs and fireflies put
up the lighting. The sunflowers captured sunlight
and turned it into electricity for the Stadium and the
Action stages. The beavers built dams with turbines
and windmills to power the lights when the sun was
not shining. The Electric Eel Company charged backup
batteries with energy from the tides. The natural world
and the Lil Gorilla worked long hours to get the stadium
ready for opening day. The stage was half-land, half-
water. Sun lit the stage by day, and Moon by night.

Meanwhile, questions still circulated across the ocean
news channels:

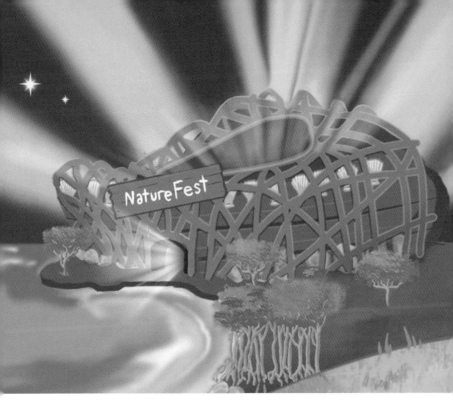

Will Pacha Jamma solve all the problems of the world?

Slithering,
  whistling,
    popping,
      rocking ...

Will these wild animals get everything done in time?

Rolling,
  roaring,
    beating,

shaking ...

Will anyone even come?

Squawking,

crinkling,

locking,

cooing,

mooing ...

All of Nature came... wing by wing, hoof-by-hoof, leaf by leaf! Every kind of species migrated into the stadium from all directions. The turtles, snails and slugs were the last to arrive — late as usual. The entire planet came — except for the humans. Pacha was so thrilled she felt like she had butterflies in her stomach. Then real butterflies flew over the stage, painting the sky with their colorful wings. With that, finally, opening day had come and the show was ready to begin!

"YEEEEEEAAAAAAAA!!!"

9

Welcome to Pacha Jamma!

The wild crowd went even wilder as the whale spouted from the underwater stage, "Welcome to PACHA JAMMA, the greatest earth festival ever! We're in tough times...we're struggling to survive...but that's why we need to come together to change the tide! When we're all connected we can halt the destruction of our planet. So, just to show everyone that we're serious about changing the future, let's make the biggest wave ever!"

Jag leapt onto the stage and led the crowd in a massive wave around the roaring stadium. The fierce cat smiled wider than Pacha had ever seen. He jumped forward, stepping out of his seriousness for a second, howling to the audience, "We are here to laugh, boogie and become friends with all of our relations! The performers are as old as 4 billion years and as young as a single day. Please enjoy the music and messages from all of the plants, animals and Nature! From near and far, across the seven seas, braving fiery deserts, storms and famine ... over the mountains, through the woods and even past grandma's house... we have arrived!"

The Lil Gorilla couldn't believe her eyes. There were so many wondrous sights and sounds ...

A dolphin breakdancin' ...
Termites and woodpeckers played mouth-drums ...
A fish circus of sole fish flipping across the waters...
An octopus singing octaves and mixing 8 songs at once
...
A duck-billed platypus stage diving ...
Bananas going BANANAS ...
A black eyed pea doing the winnowing dance ...
And a Beaver named Juston Time was singing too ...

Whale spouted water on the Lil Gorilla while announcing the next act:

"Without further ado...everyone...please join the amazing rapper, MC Plat, our choir of coral reefs and a live Lotus Band in singing Welcome to PACHA JAMMA!" As Pacha shuffled in place, rehearsing her speech in her head, she laughed about this little platypus spinning on his beak.

After the welcome song, Jag introduced the Lil Gorilla as the host of the Action Stages. This was the moment Pacha

had feared. She would be so embarrassed if the audience didn't like her. But when her PJs shimmied her hips forward, she walked on stage like a bee drunk on honey. The stadium was glittering with a billion rainbow-colored lights and creatures swaying into the distance. At that moment, time seemed to freeze as she took in the sheer magic that surrounded her.

The stadium was split in half by water and by land. The water-world of oceans and rivers splashed out in all directions to her right side while the terrestrial world of mountains and plains drifted off to her left like a giant Zen painting. All six kingdoms of animals were present --- from the reptiles, avians, mammals, and insects on her stage left to the mollusk, arthopod, and chordate families on her stage right.

The fungus and plant kingdoms were so vast and beautiful that it boggled Pacha's brain. The stadium was a patchwork of species groups, all bunched together in their micro-habitats. Giant ice-sculptures formed the stands for where the penguins, polar bears and microbes (burrowing in the icy glacial deposits) slid around. Tens of thousands of species of ferns, lichen, and moss screamed like little children after seeing a celebrity!

Pacha saw turquoise waterfalls lit up with phosphorescent dancers, turning the freshwater streams to glittery disco-ball bubble parties! She marveled at how blue-green algae, wild sponges and phytoplankton were hugging anchovy and sardine fishes, all taking a night off from eating their favorite aquatic salads. Majestic flower gardens and wildflower fields formed terrestrial bleachers in the stadium hilltops. When the wind picked up, thousands of coconut trees tossed watery refreshments across the stadium!

A giant arena of bamboo swayed in perfect harmony with a humungous underwater seaweed forest. Hundreds of flocks of colorful macaws, flamencos and hummingbirds, all hovered in mid-air above center stage. A tomato patch rooted at the base of the stadium bleachers; they were ready to jump on stage if anyone had a bad performance! Even creatures Pacha used to be scared of, like the giant squid or anaconda, were being peaceful in this moment!

Being on mainstage was a growth moment for Pacha, beautiful and scary at the same time. But surprising herself, she took a deep breath and eagerly accepted the mic.

"Lemme hear you all ... go wild!"

She listened as countless noises of the jungle roared in their own strange languages. She wasn't sure if they were happy or just crazy, but she kept going anyway:

"Gorillas in the house! Let me hear the big cats! What about trumpeting elephants and howling wolves? Where my dogs at? What does the fox say? Oh, and if you're a bird, remember to tweet #PACHAJAMMA..."

The Lil Gorilla continued, "Thank you all for coming! I know many of you came a long way to hear some of your favorite music ... but PACHA JAMMA is much more than that! Our planet earth is no longer safe and many of us feel scared, in danger, even angry sometimes."

She paused and let her words sink in with the crowd. "Maybe PACHA JAMMA is a way to change all our problems at once?"

Randomly, a bunch of troublemakers in the crowd yelled, "Can you shut up already and get the party started?!"

When these hecklers finally quieted down, the Lil Gorilla bravely continued, sharing about the action stages and teams. She invited everyone to visit the stage of their home habitats, and to join an action team. Awkwardly, the crowd still responded with much less enthusiasm than she had hoped for.

As if her worries came true, she tripped up on her final words and accidently snorted like a hog! This angered a wild pig, who immediately rushed the stage through the giraffe-guards' long legs. He spat towards the Lil Gorilla, tossing his head and oinking at her for dishonoring his species! The Lil Gorilla jumped away from the wild pig while the audience chuckled nervously, hoping the entire scene was a bad joke. As the cameras flashed, the Lil Gorilla sheepishly ran off stage, feeling humiliated.

Pacha found a tidal pool to relax in alone and figure out her next moves. Floating on her back in the warm seawater, she rehashed what had just happened over and over in her mind. She regretted not standing up for herself. Never again she told herself.

Suddenly, a giant fin appeared in front of her! Scared, she splashed onto a rock near the shore. As the fin got closer, Pacha freaked out until remembering that panic just makes things worse. The fin came directly toward her and a smiling shark surfaced with a plastic soda bottle on his tongue. He nudged the bottle toward the Lil Gorilla; he had found it in an ocean current on his way to the show. He also told her that, for future reference, sharks don't even like the taste of primates! Not knowing

what else to do, she smiled and grabbed the bottle while the shark swam away.

Sure enough, there was a message in the bottle! She twisted off the cap, and used a stick to pull out a piece of parchment paper. The message looked to be gibberish words around images of a cat, two sheep - each with funny symbols or signs next to them - and a shaggy mammal she did not recognize. For some reason, the mysterious message gave Pacha a bad feeling.

10

Message in a Bottle

Pacha rushed toward the Main Stage to find her friends. She found Hum in a bird "Nesting & Resting" area behind the dressing rooms. Sitting in the grass to catch her breath, Pacha told the jittery bird about the message the shark intercepted. After contemplating the story, Hum said "Nena, Mr. Tick's prints are all over this!" seeming more upset than ever about Mr. Tick's antics. She wondered aloud, "If anyone was going to mess with PACHA JAMMA, what part of the festival would they target?"

She and Pacha looked at each for a moment and simultaneously they both yelled "The Action Stages" and jumped up to find more information. They set off for the massive Apple Tree that hosted PACHA JAMMA's broadcasting station so they could monitor all the action stages at once.

As the Lil Gorilla hustled to keep up with Hum, she muttered to herself "Not on my watch!" Arriving at the Apple Tree, the Lil Gorilla and Hum watched Tree-V monitors for unusual activities at the different stages.

On the River Stage, a group of amphibians were just settling into a talk sponsored by the indicator species team featuring the Director of the Hop-On-It Frog Choir, Ms. Abbey Toad. On the Forest Stage, Poison Ivy was leading the other forest guardians through a workshop on the need to limit human activities in nature and ways to stop the wrecking of the wild. On other stages, they saw ice breakers like musical chairs, laughing yoga, tai chi, and coordinated actions like letter writing.

Pacha suggested that Señor may have some ideas. They found Señor in the roots below running the Interspecies Internet while helping a hackathon to make apps that improve cross-species teamwork. Like a mad scientist, Señor was connecting roots and helping vine videos grow. He was also working with popular spider websites to get the message out about what was happening at #PACHAJAMMA. Birds were tweeting in the branches above. Insects were posting and apples were computing all the information. PACHA JAMMA was going viral!

Upon hearing the Lil Gorilla's news, a visibly disturbed Señor pulled up a series of cool charts showing what was happening on all the different online networks. The animals poured over the monitor for a good time. As with any Big Data scene, it was difficult to see patterns at the beginning. Hence, Señor did quick changes to show "stories" in the data.

On one of the charts that showed information about the parasites network, Pacha saw an alarming growth of activity over the past several weeks. Hum immediately told the others, "I knew it! What is that crazy tick up to?" Señor called over the captain of the underground team – a nearsighted mole named Revere, and asked her to focus the entire team on hacking into Mr. Tick's computer system. Revere scampered off with her rodent buddies into the root tunnels where they might tap into the parasite network. Pacha passed the time pondering the animals and symbols on the message from the bottle.

After about an hour, Revere returned saying that they were able to access the parasite network but that Mr. Tick's computer had strong security and that they would need days, if not weeks, to break in. Pacha thought out loud, "But we don't have days or weeks..." and offhandedly asked Revere what she made of the symbols next to the sheep on the message.

Revere couldn't place the symbols but thought they looked human, so she opened up a wormhole to the Internet saying, "Symbols are one of the most powerful ways that humans understand each other. I've been seeing a lot of animal and plant networks adopt them, especially the emoji." Revere dragged the two icons to the Image search and both times the search showed many versions of a single circle drawn around both symbols. "Let's see! Wikipedia tells us that it's called a Yin and Yang... it's about how opposite forces are actually interconnected and in balance. **Yin** is associated with negative, feminine and the moon while **yang** is associated with positive, masculine and the sun!"

Suddenly, Pacha remembered a school trip to a local farm. She figured that the Yang sheep must be a Ram while the Yin sheep must be a Ewe!

Now all they had to do was figure out the last animal in the message, or so they thought. The team decided that Señor would monitor the grasslands and savannah biome stages for the mystery animal. Revere and her team would see what they could find on the biome networks. Hum would do flyovers of the different stages. And the Lil Gorilla would find Jag who—as organizer of the **Organization Of Organized Organisms**—would almost certainly be able to help her identify the final animal.

She found the big cat taking break from the stadium in a grassy meadow. Jag rubbed his furry chin as the Lil Gorilla told him about the message in the bottle, a cat, a yang ram, a yin ewe, and Mr. Tick's computer, until she rolled out the message.

"That's a wildebeest! I saw one at the Savannah Stage sitting in on a meeting. They might still be there. Gotta go!" Jag then bounded off, rushing back to the Main stage to officiate the Nature Superhero contest.

Even though Pacha now knew all the animals, she was at a loss for what to do. She found herself strolling off into the forest remembering that her papa said "taking a walk" helps you think clearly. But she felt no closer to solving the puzzle than a thousand steps ago. As she walked she hardly noticed that the trees and brush were actively clearing a path for her. And before she knew it, she was standing in front of Tree, who was swaying in the wind .

Tree opened her eyes and whispered, "if walking is not working, perhaps mindfulness or stretching could solve your problem." Tree paused and added, "Don't just do something, sit there!" Tree then stretched her branches wide and tall, guiding the Lil Gorilla through several different yoga poses. On the final pose, Pacha had an inspiration – perhaps every animal image that's shown on the message could be replaced with the name of the animal:

Despite being unable to read the message, Pacha had a feeling that she was on the right track. And she realized, at the moment, she needed to get back to her duties at the stages.

11

Lay of the Land

Over the next two days, the Lil Gorilla visited all the stages across the different habitats and visited with scores of action teams working on the issues of the world.

On a dock at the Ocean Stage, she met with the Oil Spill Response team, which included whales, dolphins, otters and oyster mushrooms as well as the overfishing and ocean plastic teams. She was introduced to a clownfish and a mermaid, who chuckled about how popular their species had become in human movies! On the Savannah stage, she visited the Disappearing Team, full of elephants, rhinos, gorillas, and other poaching victims. On the Tundra stage, she met with the glacier tracking team of caribou and other brave deer, who talked about how the world's weather is changing.

At the Forest Stage, she met with the reforestation team, the forest guardians, and the disappearing team. While she was hanging out and listening to stories, an awesome migration of butterflies arrived from a distant land. One butterfly even rapped the story of its life cycle, sharing the hope that we can all fly away from whatever caterpillar-like greed or problems might hold us back from being free in life.

To make things even more awesome, a giant group of bear cubs backed up by their grandpa, a famous singing bear from the 1960s, sang on a song calling for everyone to wake up! The old bear's voice sounded to Pacha like an old record player.

Unfortunately, the song was a bit of a controversy, as a group of chipmunks and squirrels sleeping in the tree boughs didn't want to wake up from hibernation yet. Just then, a gang of parasites with megaphones showed up on the back of Grandpa Bear's fur. They began to heckle the bears about their revolutionary message of change and awakening. The Lil Gorilla asked them to please keep "Be Respectful!" or she'd call for the trees to sweep them out of the forest. Though they kept quiet from then on, Pacha was concerned about the hostility they had created and hoped they wouldn't cause any more problems.

After she ran off for the River Stage, she met with the indicator species, water impurity, and dam teams. They told her that contaminated water kills more humans every year than all of their wars combined. "I can only imagine what this bad water does to plants and animals!" she thought to herself, upset. At the Grassland Stage,

she met with the pollinator's team, where everyone was actually doing a special fashion show for the wildflowers and roses. Wowza!

At the Alpine Stage, she met with the conservation teams, where Pacha got a little light-headed from so little oxygen in the high altitudes. She finally stumbled off to the Cultivated Lands Stage, where they all yelled about air pollution, water contamination, soil contamination, genetic engineering and global warming. "There's NO I IN TEAM!" they yelled, angry about how disconnected everything had become! At the Desert Stage, she met with the desertification, mining, and erosion teams where they talked mostly about what's next after the festival finishes.

At the Jungle Stage, Pacha met with the "Primates for Pachamama" teams. She looked around at the Jungle stage for signs of the "Parasites for Pachamama" team, but realized that the viruses were far too small for her to see without a microscope. Pacha also looked around for the mysterious wildebeest but no one seemed to know who that was.

Through her travels among the stages, Pacha got a lay of the land and a much fuller sense of the how large PACHA JAMMA was now that everyone had settled in. The stadium was at the center of the festival grounds where the habitats converged. Each habitat had its own stage surrounded by its own mini-festival run by huge volunteer crews. Here the inhabitants camped, fed themselves, made and traded crafts, got child care, and relaxed when they were not at the stadium or visiting the other areas.

Pacha quickly discovered that mini-festivals in the various areas were very different. She felt most at home in the Forest Fair, which was situated in a magical old-growth forest. The great horned owl from the Deforestation team meeting told her the forest was preserved by something called a "Land Trust" around the turn of the 20th century. Paths lined with food and craft booths curved through the forest. Stages hosted performances of all types from music to theater to spoken word.

And everywhere Pacha looked there were trees. In all her life, she had never experienced or imagined anything quite like it. It was a kaleidoscope of plants and animals. Nothing stood out because there was something everywhere you looked. Every 100 feet she walked, she'd see something that blew her mind!

She ran into belly-dancers, drum circles, sudden parades that anyone could join, fortune tellers, poetry slams, storytellers, vaudeville acts, stilt walkers and much more, A meadow for young plants and animals had face painting, puppet shows, hula hooping, juggling, circus acts, and other performances.

Everyone here was respectful and respected, which was very different from Pacha's school. In fact, Pacha witnessed some of the most beautiful friendships blossom at the fair. It seemed like everyone knew they were connected to each other and the forest.

Pacha found the food in the Forest Fair like no diner or restaurant she had ever seen. There was chia fudge brownies, almond butter omelets, hempnut cookies, tempeh burgers, spinach apple turnovers, organic kettle corn, kale smoothies, coconut ice cream, and veggie sushi! "Now say that 10 times fast!" giggled Pacha. She discovered that the best booths had the longest lines.

Late at night, once the larger groups were shooed-out, the REAL party began. The fair turned into a city of lights and sights. Only fair volunteers, performers, artisans, food vendors, and organizers like Pacha who had ALL PACHA JAMMA passes were allowed to stay.

For the first time since she had been in this strange and wonderful land, Pacha noticed the stars. They were so much brighter than the city. Up until then, she hadn't a chance to take a breather or relax. She finally let go and embraced the moment. She could not imagine a better movie than just sitting back and watching the stars form characters and stories in the sky.

A shooting star made her remember the stories her abuelita told her about origin of the universe, and her mama saying that we are all stardust becoming aware of our connectedness. Pacha made a wish that she would be able to fully experience her connection with her namesake, Pachamama. Being there, Pacha had the sense that everything was living in a natural world order and that PACHA JAMMA was part of its evolution. But each habitat was totally unique. For example, she got an entirely different feeling at the hot and dry Desert habitat, which was more like the festival her father always talked about called Burning Man. Though she still regretted her performance on the mainstage, she was actually happy with her performance as Action Stage Leader!

12

Monkey Traps

As she ate breakfast the next day, Pacha had the message on her mind. She whistled for Hum who happened to be nearby. Pacha mentioned her conversation with Jag. Hum hadn't seen the mystery animal and zipped off to take another look.

Minutes later, Hum whizzed back and hovered in front of Pacha. "The mystery animal is headed to the Savannah Stage now but I have to go to the Grasslands Stage for a Pollinators meeting." Knowing that pollinators were big time gossipers, Pacha decided to tag along. Maybe they had picked up some news as they went from flower to flower.

As they approached the stage, the buzzing was over-whelming for Pacha. She remembered the time her mother had to tweeze out the stinger of a bee that Pacha accidently stepped on at the park. Although the sting hurt, she felt more sorry for the bee than anything else. While she wasn't really scared of bees, a part of her was deathly afraid of wasps. And remembering this about herself, she started to turn around and go back, but Hum reminded her that all of nature had signed a truce for the duration of PACHA JAMMA. Pacha was a little skeptical that the truce extended to humans but Hum assured her that it covered PACHA JAMMA. After all, Hum exclaimed, if not, wouldn't a mountain lion or jaguar have eaten her by now?

During the pollinators meeting, Pacha shared her confusions with the bees and wasps. They looked at the partially decrypted message with confusion. One bee suggested that Mr. Tick's way of thinking is so backwards, and he really needs to change. At that, Pacha realized that the words in the message are all backwards!

She then unscrambled the message:

At my mark
jewel wasp attack
jtseebedliwle stage,
final night.

One of the wise old lady wasps said the jewel wasps were a cult of brain-controlling wasps. Pacha was horrified to learn that one sting could turn mammals into zombies. Not good news but at least Pacha had a sense of what they were up against. No one, however, had any idea what the "jtseebedliwle" meant. As Pacha prepared to

leave, the pollinator team offered to help out however
made sense. Pacha and Hum thanked them and set off
for the Savannah Stage to find the wildebeest; perhaps it
could help solve the last part of the puzzle.

As Pacha and Hum made their way, they reflected on
the day and all the back and forth between stages. They
finally arrived at the Savannah Stage just as the Wildebeest was leaving. It had been a long day and the wildebeest was ready for some down time. Pacha and Hum

told the wildebeest about the message in the bottle, how they had almost cracked the code, and the dead end they found themselves in. The tired wildebeest said it had no idea what "jtseebedliwle" meant. As the wildebeest turned to leave, on a whim, Pacha asked, "Do you have any other names?"

The wildebeest answered, "Yes, my friends call me *gnu*."

Pacha almost swallowed her tongue but managed to stammer.

"It's not jTSEEBEDLIWle... It's jUNGle... the jungle stage is their attack target!"

Feeling both triumph and fear, Pacha raced after Hum, who had darted off to the Jungle Stage to warn the primates about the attack. But no one was around. Just as they were about to call security, Hum noticed a bunch of bonobos and monkeys high in the branches above watching Tree-V. Through leaves, branches and primate hair, the Lil Gorilla saw a human girl bravely speaking on behalf of the rocks, trees and waters at another earth festival! The primates were happy to see that there might be some humans that could be trusted.

The Lil Gorilla excitedly climbed up to the canopy and blurted out "I bet there are other kids that want to help nature too." The primates laughed, saying that there would likely be so few, it'd take a miracle to make a difference in the world.

A monkey with a floppy hat and a pipe said "We know that there will soon be millions, if not billions, of humans ready for our Coming Home To Nature program. We just need a way to reach a lot of humans with the right message! If only one major celebrity would join our cause! Most of us think the answer lies in connecting our primate network (and eventually the rest of nature) into the human Internet." He paused thoughtfully.

"Maybe then we can meet on the same level as earthlings and be a mirror for them? What I like most is, they will only know you're a monkey or an ape if you choose to tell them! Using this Internet, through music and stories, we can change the dream of humanity!"

He slapped his knee and exclaimed "Wow! That could really be something..." as the rest of the primates hooted in a mix of confusion and excitement.

"I don't mean to put a damper on things, but..." The Lil Gorilla interrupted to tell them about the wasp attack. The primates hollered and beat their chests, ready to defend themselves and *PACHA JAMMA*. A female chimp interrupted the posturing to suggest that they consider non-violence but the male primates quickly lost interest and began chest bumping.

The Lil Gorilla, however, got their attention when she said one sting from a jewel wasp could turn the most alpha primate into a hapless zombie, which took much of the bluster out of their boast. She then suggested that they form a new action team to stop the attack on the Jungle Stage, and asked that the primates lead the recruiting so she could get back to her duties as Action Stage Leader. The primates agreed, Hum flew off, and Pacha scampered off towards the main stage to give her next update.

As she walked, Pacha felt a raindrop and then another and another. She wondered if a storm might be coming. "Well, we need the rain right? It could fun maybe...like frolicking in a water park!" thought Pacha. She tried to catch raindrops with her tongue but there weren't enough to satisfy her growing thirst. She needed something refreshing to cool and calm her down.

Pacha found herself looking for coconuts in a nearby grove. She recalled watching her abuelita chop the top off of a coconut like a fruit ninja, drinking the coconut water, and then scooping out the meat with a piece of the husk. If only she had her abuelita's machete. Surprisingly, Pacha noticed what looked like a freshly opened coconut. Upon further inspection, however, she realized that the water was gone and the coconut was tied to a stake.

"Does everything have to be a riddle?!" Thought Pacha, annoyed. Even worse, the coconut was directly under a worrisome pile of ticks high above on a branch. She was about to drop the coconut when she noticed something shiny inside. She thrust her hand in the hole to grab the shiny thing, but try as she might, she couldn't wrangle it out.

When Pacha looked up, she saw dozens of chubby ticks slowly rappelling towards her on tiny rope ladders. She knew that they meant no good. But she couldn't pull her attention far enough away from the shiny thing to do anything differently. When she held the shiny thing, Pacha felt a weird twist in her tummy. Not really a bad feeling, but it didn't feel good either.

As if coming out of a fog, she realized that her PJ arms were pressing on her inner wrist, which made her want to let go. Pacha was confused. She felt a new sense of danger as her hand began to hurt and her breath grew short.

Pacha's attachment to having the shiny thing was strong, but she trusted her PJs. Finally, when she accepted that she was not going to have the shiny thing, her belly felt better! Pacha dropped the coconut, and stepped away just the pile of ticks fell directly on the coconut screaming in frustration. She shook her head, stuck her tongue out and hightailed away from the monkey trap.

13

The Storm

Feeling like she dodged a catastrophe, Pacha made her way back to the mainstage at the stadium in time to see some green chili peppers and komodo dragons perform. Shortly after she arrived however, it started raining cats and dogs. Not real cats and dogs, of course, but tons of rain showering down. At first, many cheered alongside the desert, savanna and grasslands dwellers, who were in a long drought. But as the storm picked up momentum, murmurs of worry traveled across the stadium. Like dominos, the frogs sounded an alarm across the stadium: "Change Climate Change Ribbit! Change Climate Change Ribbit!"

A windstorm blew in like a greedy and out-of-control goblin. Screeching through the crowds, the wind knocked out one of the largest stadium lights, sending the moths into frenzy. The security "O-fish-als" noticed the tide was rising quickly. By then, everyone was running for cover. Mothers comforted their babies as they dove underground, swam underwater, squeezed inside tree bark, or huddled into buffalo circles.

After the wind died down and everyone returned to the stadium, the loudspeakers blared a public service message, saying that the PACHA JAMMA festival was in the eye of the hurricane and now a superstorm was heading their direction!

Everything went totally silent and calm. Sadly, that moment lasted only a moment. A huge lightning bolt lit up the sky, followed almost immediately by a monstrous thunderclap and the onset of a torrential downpour.

Frantic animals stampeded the exits. Hum whizzed up to Pacha, yelling "Follow me or you'll get crushed!"

The Lil Gorilla raced behind the bird, dipping and bobbing through the stormy crowd. Following Hum's lead, she barely managed to grab hold of a thrashing branch from a large tree. Pulling herself up into the branches, she could see a river of animals being swept down and out toward the torrential ocean waves crashing against the stadium seating. She watched as animals tried to escape through the stadium exits.

When Hum and Pacha finally made their way out of the stadium they ran into Grandpa bear and his grand-cubs. The Lil Gorilla was smitten with the little cubs and worried about how they would fare the storm. Sensing

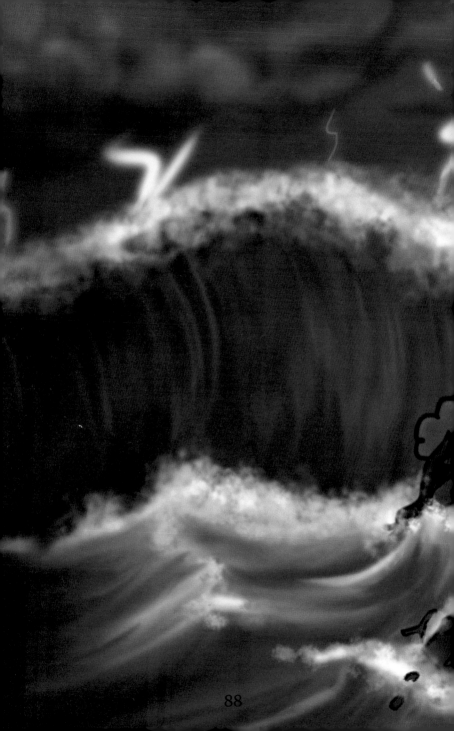

the old bear's skittishness, she asked whether he had a safe place for them to spend the night. He nodded and said they were headed to his old hibernating grounds - the caves in the mountains between the Temperate Forest Stage and the Tundra Stage - but worried about getting the agitated cubs to the caves at night with this hurricane raging.

The Lil Gorilla rounded up some friends and they all set off. Following the old bear's lead, the Lil Gorilla, Hum, Plat, Jag, and a friendly cobra corralled and proceeded to march the bear cubs into the mountains to find cover for the night. The procession went well, considering that they were often on muddy mountain goat trails in the middle of the night, with rain pounding down on them.

Thankfully, Grandpa Bear found the opening to cave larger than the theater at Pacha's school. When they arrived, they took a moment of silence to give thanks for their good fortune. As Pacha surveyed the space, she noticed that the cave had three openings leading deeper into the mountain. The thought of exploring them made her tingle with curiosity. But getting some rest was a priority.

Safe and dry in the cave, the Lil Gorilla helped the animals set up leafy beds and twiggy nests using materials they found laying around. In short order, many of animals drifted off to sleep and that's when the noise started. The cave echoed with animal snores! Unable to sleep, the Lil Gorilla was contemplating what do, when Plat waddled over to her. They talked about the unfortunate snoring situation and decided to see if they could find some quiet in one of the tunnels. But which tunnel?

Plat pointed at each tunnel in sequence as he flowed:

Eenie meanie miney moe
Catch a tick tack by the toe
When he hollers, don't let him go
My mama told me be brave
when you enter this cave!

Plat was pointing at the middle tunnel. They cautiously entered, Plat leading the way. The Lil Gorilla was surprised that she could see anything at all. She hadn't realized the PJs were glow-in-the-dark. As she ambled and trudged through the tunnel, Pacha started thinking about how they were going to get back. She wondered out loud if they should mark their trail. Plat said "Let's use what we got. How about unmmm rocks?" At each crossroad, they stacked rocks to show where they had come from.

Plat noticed it first – a faint buzzing that grew louder and louder until it was clearly a gathering of mosquitos or wasps, which got the Lil Gorilla a little nervous. As they moved forward stealthily, they heard a sinister cackling. But when Plat asked if she wanted to turn back, the Lil Gorilla said no. As they slinked forward, the tunnel opened up into a large hallway connected to the source of the noise – the board room in Mr. Tick's lair!

MC Plat hopped onto a small crate to peek through the window on the door with Pacha. They heard Mr Tick giving a presentation about preventing future PACHA JAMMAs. He showed a map of the entire festival grounds and described how wasp attack at the Jungle Stage was the first in a series of attacks that would grow into a species war, and ultimately "break this silly truce!" He then presented a slide showing the explosion of human population over the past 10,000 years from less than 10 million to 7 billion! He then showed how this mirrored the growth amongst parasites. In that moment, Pacha realized that Mr. Tick and his minions were trying to keep the world the same for themselves.

Pacha was outraged at their selfishness! Despite her desire to disrupt the meeting, she restrained Plat from going after Mr. Tick, reminding him about the jewel wasps.

But unfortunately Plat tripped over his feet and slipped off the crate he was standing on, waking up a giant wasp in a security uniform. The wasp's grogginess shifted into a snarl, and he dove towards the Lil Gorilla.

At the last moment, Plat knocked the Lil Gorilla out of the wasp's path. The wasp whizzed past the Lil Gorilla, hit and then slid down the wall. As the security wasp lay on the ground unconscious, they noticed a strange smell emanating from him. Recalling a science lesson, the Lil Gorilla said, "He's releasing something called "pheromones", which will call his brain-controlling wasp friends! We can't stay here!"

As Pacha and Plat sprinted out of Mr. Ticks lair, the buzzing grew louder into yelps, which seemed to follow them at every turn. At each crossroad, they retraced their path thanks to their rock piles, which they dismantled as they went along. Pacha didn't feel safe until they arrived back at the cave with her animal friends. To their surprise, the cave was much quieter than before. The Lil Gorilla gave Plat a hug "good night" and settled into her bed of leaves.

14

A Song of Hope

But Pacha still couldn't sleep. Maybe it was the storm of emotions she was feeling. Disappointed that she hadn't stopped Mr Tick. Spooked by the dreaded jewel wasps. Unsettled by the destructive weather. Feeling unseen for her true self in the Gorilla mask.

She stayed up all night thinking about how to stop the wasps. She remembered what Tree taught her. As she did breathwork, she thought about the how humans have been acting like parasites and parasites like humans because they "never think about anything but themselves and the next day's food." She wondered if that's what is really causing the storm, the problems in nature and even her health problems. She imagined that humans everywhere might be in a big monkey trap. Pacha

thanked herself for staying strong, no matter how tough the journey might be.

Early in the morning, Pacha remembered Mama telling her that that the darkest night is always followed by dawn. With the first light, she went to the mouth of the cave to survey the damage. The storm had destroyed the entire stadium! But, Pacha focused her mind on seeing PACHA JAMMA unite the biosphere and alter the course of the planet.

Out of nowhere, she felt a song in her heart. She began to sing a soft lullaby, feeling the healing energy of the music pulse through her body. A little tree frog joined her, croaking a beautiful melody. Sixteen bars later, a couple more frogs and Ms. Abby Toad joined. Soon a giant orchestra of frogs, toads and birds was harmonizing across the entire riparian world. With happiness welling up in her eyes, Pacha watched the clouds part and begin to melt away! Sunlight shined through the retreating storm clouds, spreading love through the cave, across the festival grounds, through the biomes! The sound of music brought peace to the land and seas, calming all beings, from smallest to largest.

As the light spread, the animals and plants awakened to a new joy for life. "No matter what, life keeps on living!" thought Pacha, amazed. The creatures embraced, happy to have survived the storm of the century. The animal, mineral and vegetable kingdoms honored the moment by bringing a gift of gratitude to an ever-widening circle of beings. Each gift was placed into a mandala honoring those who had fallen in defense of Pachamama. Looking around this giant circle of life, everyone seemed stronger than ever! The natural world had bonded and strengthened as a result of the hurricane.

Thanks to the dams built by the beavers and meerkats, the major leaks were plugged. Once the stadium area was dry, the ants, bees, termites, and other crafty critters sang works songs as they rebuilt the broken walls, fixed the water damage, and replanted the flower gardens. To help with erosion, millions of seeds popped up from underground, singing: "We used to be underground artists but now we're pop stars!" The monkeys, elephants and hippos partnered to lift up the toppled trees. A giraffe and a crane used their long necks to help put the signs back up while the electric eels repowered the lights.

As the jungle reunited, the Lil Gorilla joined the crowds in the mud and muck, cleaning and fixing. It took many hours, but the hard work finally returned the stadium to its original beauty. Trumpeting elephants announced that the festival was set to resume. Monkeys with air horns called the scaredy-cats back from hiding. Pacha felt excited walking to the stadium when she saw a herd of baby hippos squealing, "I'm excited. I'm excited..."

Pacha noticed that everyone was excited, except probably Mr. Tick who was certainly furious that the storm hadn't put an end to PACHA JAMMA. Mr. Tick would probably have been hopeless had he not more tricks up his sleeve. She imagined him drooling with delight, thinking about his wasp attack on the Jungle stage taking out the Primate team. For him, it was absolutely necessary that they turn the other species against the primates and shut down this dangerous festival to change the dream of humanity.

Then, for some reason, Pacha thought about what it must be like to be in Mr. Tick's little shoes. Surely Mr. Tick seemed very loyal to his parasites. He obviously was trying to make things better for his family. Who could blame him for that? But when it comes at the expense of Pachamama and web of life, Pacha thought "Not here, not now."

Pacha wished she could be excited as the others but she was worried about Mr. Tick's brain-controlling wasp attack, which could prevent PACHA JAMMA from ever happening again! She was looking forward to recon-necting with the primates and the new team they were

putting together to thwart the Jungle Stage attack. But for now, she realized, the show must go on.

When everyone arrived, there was a feeling that PACHA JAMMA was even stronger than ever. Crowds poured back into the stadium, ready for the fun to begin again. Entire classes of animals - like the amphibia, mammalia and reptilia - were hugging and kissing like a big family reunited!

The Lil Gorilla buoyed the crowd with the progress of the action teams. She resisted mentioning Mr. Tick's attack because she didn't want to freak out the crowd. Mama would often say some things are better left unsaid. She handed off to MC Plat, who lit up the crowd with his sweet self-love song "Use What You Got." The beaver named Juston Time then brought the stadium to tears with his love rap, "Water Baby." After which, Sir Elephant wowed the crowd with his spoken word about bringing dreams to life.

Pacha was enjoying the vibes. She was excited to see her friend Señor come to the stage with a bevy of backup singers. Señor taught the crowd the chorus while the Lil Gorilla and two Flamingos taught them the Connected Dance. Following his lead, the crowd practiced a couple of times. Señor then said "Drop that Beat! "

The entire stadium sung the "We Are ALL Connected" chorus and Señor even did a fresh rap on the verses. Afterwards he spoke about how all beings are connected through Pachamama, the web of life, our shared destiny. He stressed the importance of working together even when everything seems to want to pull us apart. That's why the truce is so important. Pacha got chills down her spine when he said "Just as we rebuilt this stadium, we can rebuild the world, as long as we do it together." In closing, Señor spoke of a time when all of nature's children would dance together for the earth! Perhaps on Earth Day.

15

Stop, Rock and Roll!

While everyone was hugging and prepping for the next performers on stage, the Lil Gorilla told Señor: "I don't mean to be a downer, but Mr. Tick is still out there, and he is planning an attack on the Jungle stage to break the truce! The last thing he wants is for us all to be connected..."

The mushroom turned red with anger. When he calmed down, he checked in with his friends in the mycelium network. They suggested Pacha enroll Pebble and his rock friends in the action team for stopping the attack.

Nervous, they went poking around in some boulders. In a pile of rocks, they found Pebble cracking jokes. When Pebble heard the news, he suggested that they should be patient, as the President of the United States of

AmeRocka would be arriving soon. It was his special gift to the festival on behalf of the mineral kingdom. Not only that, he said, but "wherever the President shows up, the entire mineral kingdom shows up too."

Sure enough, within a quarter turn of the sun, Mr. President arrived at the stadium with hundreds of stones following him for autographs. Mr. President even took a picture with Pebble, thanking him for all his hard work and the invitation to PACHA JAMMA. "Imagine that!", thought Pacha! "An ordinary sandstone getting respect from the greatest rock in the history of rocks!" The President also posed with other rock stars like Ruby, who was preparing for a performance herself.

As Pebble, Señor, and the Lil Gorilla marched their way down to the main stage, they could hear Mr. President take the stage. As he spoke, a huge roar swept across the stadium and the earth shook. While the crowd chanted and rocked out, the Lil Gorilla asked Pebble if he would join the action team to stop the wasps. Pebble wasn't sure what rocks could do to stop wasps but agreed to try to get some of his rock brothers to come.

After the President left, Ruby backed by Emerald and Gold sung "It's All Love", a song about the feeling of love that was in the air at PACHA JAMMA.

Afterwards, Jag roared and Wilder breeched as they took the stage, thanking everyone for a great day, Pacha felt a flurry of conflicting emotions. She was feeling worried and excited, as well as connected and disconnected (because she still was still posing as a gorilla). She paused for a moment, breathing and stretching. The planned attack would soon be on them and Pacha braced herself for a battle. She paused for a moment to notice the changes in her body. Her breath was shallow, her heartbeat rapid, and her face was sweatier than a hot dancefloor under her mask. She really wanted to take the mask off, but fear of how she would be received kept it on.

For the first time, she felt uncomfortable in her PJs. She asked herself, "How do I want to be right now?" But answers did not come. So she asked herself, "What story do I want to tell Mama and Papa about now when I get home?" It was about then that her inner warrior kicked in! She saw that everything, even flubbing her speech, was a lesson preparing her for this very moment. She smiled inside, feeling comfortable in her PJs again. She was thankful that the primates had taken the lead on getting help, and eager to do whatever she could to help.

The next day, Pebble, Plat and the Lil Gorilla went to the Jungle Stage to meet the primates. Much to their chagrin, only a third of the primates and a handful of rocks showed up. The wise old chimp explained that most of the primates were recovering from a blowout after-party at the Jungle stage. And apparently the other critters they had invited had forgotten about the meeting as well. Pacha was surprised and disappointed that the animals weren't taking this more seriously.

Just when the Pacha was about to say something, she realized that a Palo Santo tree and three huge Australian tree ferns had joined the group, somehow without her even noticing. And then a contingent of stones skipped over to the gathering. Her heart fluttered open when Hum zipped up.

The Lil Gorilla addressed the group, "Thank you so much for coming. As you know, Mr. Tick is planning a wasp attack on the Jungle Stage during tomorrow's Primate Games." The Palo Santo spoke up, "Mr. Tick wants to break the truce and keep the web of life divided. But PACHA JAMMA, and the primate's effort to change the dream of humanity, is challenging the story he is selling the parasite network. That is why he is coming after the Jungle Stage!"

The Lil Gorilla chimed in, "Well said! Who has some ideas?" And continued when no one spoke up, "Don't all speak at once. Seriously, we need a plan." One of the rocks said, "Frankly, I'm only here because of Pebble. I don't know anything about insects." One of the tree ferns spoke up, "You saw how slow we move; I don't know how we'd help stop those speedy wasps." A couple of rocks even skipped off. Pacha winced and imagined Mr. Tick cackling like he did in the cave. She could tell that, like her, most of the primates were terrified by this situation.

Some of the younger orangutans, however, told of painful encounters with regular wasps. One suggested that the tree ferns donate their largest fronds to make giant fly – er, wasp – swatters but no one thought that would work.

It was then that Plat spoke up, "Each and every one of you has a different gift! Trees are tall, rocks are hard, hummingbirds are fast flyers, Palo Santo is aromatic, mushrooms are great communicators, primates are smart (when they are not being dumb), and platypuses, I mean platypi, are very adaptable." Plat saw some smiles. "I don't have a clue what exactly we should do but I do know this" and he proceeded to sing "Use What You Got."

The other animals started clapping, singing the choruses with Plat and doing the Duck Dance. Pacha thought to herself, "these crazy critters never miss a chance to party."

After taking a bow, Plat continued, "You each have every-thing you need within yourself. You are whole, perfect and complete. And together we have everything we need to create the world we want to live in. We just need to figure out how our gifts can work together to serve the highest good ... that is, protecting the truce, PACHA JAMMA, and Pachamama!"

Pacha was glowing inside. Plat's talk reminded her of what her abuelita used to say and how she used Palo Santo. "Thanks Plat! I think I have an idea and it involves all of us. But I need some time to map it all out. Unless you hear differently, everyone meet me here at the Jungle Stage tomorrow afternoon. And primates, please bring as many of your friends as possible. Same goes to rocks and trees. Hum, please ask the bees and wasps to come. Señor, please bring me two bags of red clay tomorrow."

As the plants and animals made their way, the Lil Gorilla stayed back to survey the stage. The Jungle Stage was actually a theater in the round, featuring a circular stage surrounded by many circles of seats, none further than 50 feet from the stage. The stage had the ability to rotate in either direction and change speeds. The entire theater was surrounded by large redwood and sequoia trees with hemp rope platforms that served as balcony seating and wooden treehouses for the alpha males and their mates. Pacha did a full sketch of the stage on a piece of Papyrus.

16

Use What You Got

That night was a restless one for Pacha. She stayed up late planning and plotting the defense of the Jungle Stage. And even when she wanted to go to sleep, the ideas kept on coming. When she finally calmed her mind, she had a vision of her abuelita offering encouragement and kind words. She knew she was on the right track and fell fast asleep.

When she arrived at Jungle Stage that afternoon with Hum, she was pleasantly surprised that the entire team showed up with family. They were 108 primates, over 300 rocks, 12 fern trees, 6 Palo Santo, and thousands of bees and wasps.

Pacha was overjoyed to see Señor and his mushroom posse slide up with a bucket of red clay in tow.

"Thank you all for coming! I think we've got everything we need." She then instructed them to smear the red clay paste on each other. "My papa told me to wear red in the garden at school because most insects including bees and wasps cannot see red." It was quite amusing to watch as the critters slathered the clay on. She chuckled when some got in her mouth, and said "You are now invisible to the wasps so you don't have to worry about being stung."

Next, she asked Palo Santo trees to sacrifice their smallest branches and twigs. With the same care they use when they groom their own, the primates, under direction of Señor from below and Hum from above, trimmed the Palo Santo trees and created several hundred small bundles of the wood. The fern trees waved their fronds to cool down the clay-covered primates.

The Lil Gorilla then had the orangutan's sort out the flat and bowl shaped rocks while the chimps, bonobos, apes, and four tiny lemurs gathered moss clumps from the forest. They were careful to always ask the moss and not to take too much.

The Lil Gorilla, with Hum and Señor's assistance, then positioned primates around the outside of the Jungle Stage with two smooth stones, a bowl-shaped rock with a clump of moss, and Palo Santo bundle. She put the lemurs around the Jungle Stage and then told the primates to watch the lemurs for the signal. Next, she positioned the 12 tree ferns around stage. She had her bee and wasp friends wait in nearby trees. The Lil Gorilla, Hum, Plat and Señor each took a position around the stage so that any of them could alert the lemurs depending on the direction the jewel wasps came.

While the team was preparing, the Primate Games were in full effect. From her view, Pacha watched the end of a silly-dancing battle between a lemur and an orangutan! As the crowd cheered, Pacha heard a low hum. At first she thought it might be the crowd, but she realized that the wasps were the only ones who sounded like flying ninjas in the dark. Strangely the buzzing did not get louder. The Lil Gorilla looked to Hum, Señor and Plat. From their expressions, she understood that they all heard the low buzz but couldn't see anything unusual. Pacha locked eyes with Hum for a moment and Hum flew off to investigate.

Within in minutes, Hum frantically zipped to Pacha. "A huge cloud of wasps is circling the stage like giant donut."

Pacha was surprised and alarmed. Had there been a change in Mr. Tick's plans? She asked Hum what direction the wasps were circling and Hum said clockwise. Pacha mused, "The stage is moving clockwise as well. I bet the wasps are confused by the rotation of the stage." Mama had always taught Pacha to experiment, fail fast, and change plans if it's not working. To test her theory, the Lil Gorilla asked the stage person to change the direction of the stage to go the other way while Hum flew off to observe the wasp cloud. Sure enough, the wasps also changed the direction of their circling. "This is going to work even better than I thought!" exclaimed Pacha. The Lil Gorilla asked the stage person to keep the stage rotating for the moment.

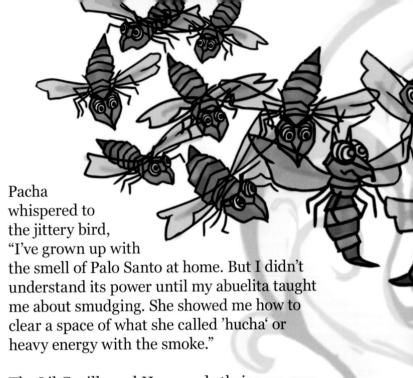

Pacha
whispered to
the jittery bird,
"I've grown up with
the smell of Palo Santo at home. But I didn't
understand its power until my abuelita taught
me about smudging. She showed me how to
clear a space of what she called 'hucha' or
heavy energy with the smoke."

The Lil Gorilla and Hum made their way over
to the Palo Santo trees, who were still recovering from giving themselves away. Pacha
thanked the Palo Santo trees again
for their help. "My intention is to
clear this Jungle Stage and the
entire PACHA JAMMA festival
of this deadly wasp hucha,
and to create a field of energy
based on connectedness and
love rather than division
and fear. Axé. Amen. Aho!"

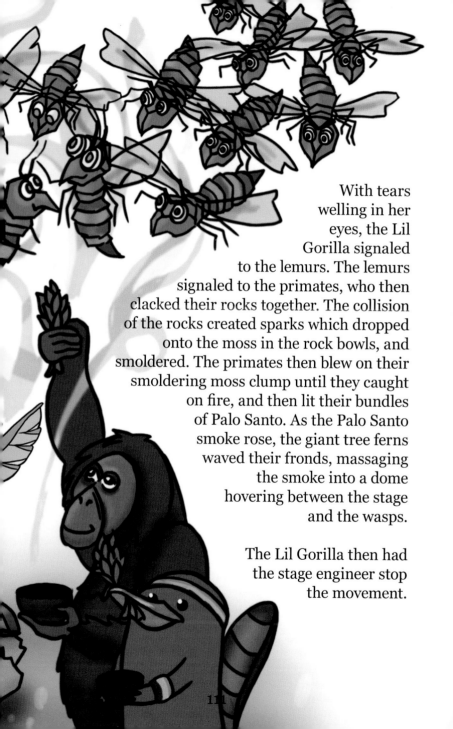

With tears welling in her eyes, the Lil Gorilla signaled to the lemurs. The lemurs signaled to the primates, who then clacked their rocks together. The collision of the rocks created sparks which dropped onto the moss in the rock bowls, and smoldered. The primates then blew on their smoldering moss clump until they caught on fire, and then lit their bundles of Palo Santo. As the Palo Santo smoke rose, the giant tree ferns waved their fronds, massaging the smoke into a dome hovering between the stage and the wasps.

The Lil Gorilla then had the stage engineer stop the movement.

Pacha watched as the donut scattered into massive waves of wasps coming from all directions. But as soon as they hit the Palo Santo smoke, they fluttered aimlessly about, falling in love with each other on the spot. Meanwhile, Hum signaled to her pollinator friends to take the love-struck jewel wasps safely away and to quickly welcome them back into the pollinator community. Pacha was so relieved that she kept her cool and that the Jungle Stage spectators didn't freak out. Afterwards, the entire team gathered to celebrate their triumph.

17

The Final Dance

The next day whizzed by for the Lil' Gorilla, as she bounced around the festival, in and out of the stadium. She was a little nervous about her performance, but much less than she might have expected. Being the last performer of the festival, she was excused from her other duties for the day and actually had a chance to spend some time in the stands. Seeing the festival from the spectator's perspective, talking to audience members and overhearing some of their conversations inspired Pacha.

She was especially excited by a conversation she overheard between the two flamingo sisters that were on stage singing the chorus of We Are All Connected. The sisters were reflecting on how the storm actually brought everyone together. When one of the sisters said the only thing missing at PACHA JAMMA was the "hairless apes", Pacha's heart skipped a beat. She got goosebumps when the pink flamingo exclaimed, "Making the world a better place is going to take ALL OF US, including the hairless apes."

The orange flamingo sighed, "I guess that'll have to wait until next year." Pacha thought to herself "maybe not."

Later that evening, a white buffalo, a snow lion and a llama appeared on-stage as if emerging from thin air! They wowed the phosphorescence photographers, who took thousands of pictures. After the photos stopped flashing and the applause started to wane, the llama spoke:

"Thank you for welcoming me. I bring greetings and congratulations from the newly constituted Council of All Beings. The new council formed organically here from the work of the Connectedness Action Team, which held listening sessions at all the different Action Stages. We found that PACHA JAMMA is truly a worldwide movement that has been emerging for decades. Billions of us share many values, which orient our lives in a common direction - regardless of our species or the habitat in which we live.

"While our practices and beliefs are many, we share knowledge about the greatest challenges to the earth and a resolve to work together to ensure a healthy planet for our species and the entire web of life. Between now and the next PACHA JAMMA, we look forward to going forward from a truce to a real treaty so we can all work with the primates on shifting the dream of humanity and healing Pachamama in full."

The Llama then announced it was time for the final performance. A grand finale with the now famous, Lil Gorilla!

Pacha was feeling the fate of the planet in her body. Her nerves now felt like they were falling off of a cliff at a thousand miles per hour. But something pushed her forward, calling her to face her fears of being seen and heard. Maybe the birds would catch her and teach her to fly? Plus, the festival had survived a super storm and a brain-controlling wasp attack ... if she didn't perform she'd be called a scaredy-cat by the lions and tigers!

Wearing starlight glitter, the Lil Gorilla stepped into the backstage while flashes from the crystal strobe lights went off everywhere. But just as the DJ Octopus queued up the track for her performance, Pacha realized something was on her shoulder! Of course, it was none other than Mr. Tick! Out of nowhere! He threatened her with all of his might:

"I'm taking your slot Lil' Ms. Wheezer! I knew you were a human from the first taste... and if you don't let me take the spotlight, I'll reveal you right now! This whole festival has been disastrous for me and it's all because of you! Consider yourself lucky that I don't chomp you like a burger right now."

Whereas in the past, she might have frozen in fear or lost her breath, Pacha closed her eyes to find her center! She tuned into her breath and straightened her spine. She

realized that she was starting to tap into an inner strength and courage that she didn't usually notice but was always there. She was feeling, er... heroic!

Pacha chose to let go of her fears. She realized that she had the power to stop this little luna-tick from stealing the joy out of life. As Mr. Tick continued blabbing threats, Pacha calmly walked over to the security area and, with the flick of her finger-nail, knocked Mr. Tick into a Venus-fly trap. The flower closed its jaws, locking Mr. Tick up in his own personal box seat. Luckily for Mr. Tick, the carnivorous flower was observing the truce like everyone else at Pacha Jamma. The Lil Gorilla told the flower to let Mr. Tick go once the show was over, to allow for him to change, like everything else in the world. As Mr. Tick screamed out in frustration, the stadium microphone announced:

"One more time, please give it up for the Lil Gorilla!"

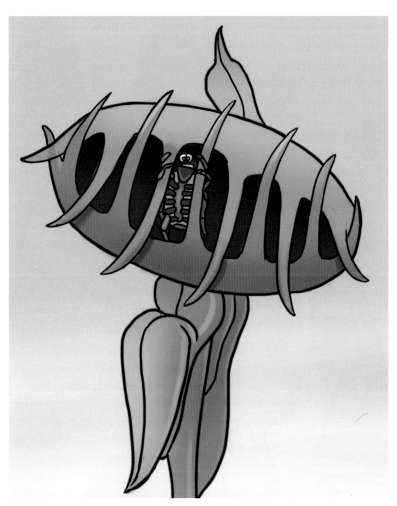

As if nothing had just happened, the Lil Gorilla did her best superstar walk out onto the stage, waving and blowing kisses. She felt more confident than ever, having stopped that wicked tick once and for all. Somehow her stage fright had finally vanished and was nowhere to be found. She was in her element!

The Lil Gorilla went on to do an "evolution of dance":

...she did the worm...
she did the funky chicken
she did the hound-dog...
she did amazing backflips
across the stage!

She did the Roger Rabbit-
The Humpty Hump...

...she did a wild version of the Monkey!
She even moonwalked in the moonlight!
The crowd went crazy in laughter
and amazement!

It was like watching
Myco Jackson for
the first time...jaw
dropping! The peanut
gallery was going nuts.

18
Who I Really Am

At the end of her dance performance, however, Pacha felt everything go into slow motion, though the audience didn't have a clue. She saw how much everyone loved her dancing and it confirmed for her, something she felt all along, that maybe she didn't need to hide behind the gorilla mask after all. "Either they love me as I am or... well... I don't want cheers for something I'm not!" thought Pacha as she came to her final dance movement.

At the last moment, the Lil Gorilla threw off her mask in a gesture of triumph. The crowd went totally silent in shock. After all, the Lil Gorilla wasn't a gorilla after all - it was the dreamer, a little Girl-illa! The audience began whispering in many languages: "...it's a human...a human in nature? A human in nature!"

Along with the whispers, Pacha heard bits of appreciations all around her. Hum and the flamingos flapping their wings, Jag clapping his paws, Tree's branches creaking, Whale breeching, Pebble cracking up and Señor whooping. More and more plants and animals joined in, and soon the entire crowd was roaring. Pacha was almost as amazed as the audience. From somewhere deep inside, she found the courage to speak her truth.

"I am a child of Nature...like all of you. Your dream is my dream too."

There was silence across the stadium.

"It's been a long journey to get here and I've faced many problems, but I'm not afraid anymore! I'm not afraid of who I am! I am Pacha!"

You could hear a feather fall and a dragonfly flap its wings. There was not a dry eye in the house. Jag stepped forward on his hind legs, putting his paw gently on Pacha's shoulder and whispered in her ear "Child, you are so much more than you know. In my tradition, the word Pacha signifies the One Life force that flows through everything. Pacha means oneness!"

At that very moment, Pacha realized that was what Señor was trying to tell her earlier with his riddle. She was to ask the teacher to "make her one with everything", and indeed he had. With teary eyes, she put her arm around the sneaky mushroom, who had slid on stage laughing.

The brawny feline then surveyed the audience and roared, "I have a dream that one day all of Nature will be honored as equal! There is no doubt in my mind that our beloved mother Pachamama loves all of you for who you are! It's a dream come true to bring together all species... Pacha being human makes this festival complete!" He smiled at Pacha and continued. "Now let's get the rest of the human family to honor the Mother Earth and stop troubling this precious home of ours. Will you dream with me? Will you dream for freedom? Let freedom sing!"

Pacha suddenly realized that Pachamama knew all along that she was human and that she was humanity's messenger. She suddenly saw how going around the world to wake up the primates and everything she did at PACHA JAMMA was just part of her journey to know herself and her gifts. For the first time she could remember, Pacha finally felt comfortable in her skin.

"I've learned from all of you that together we can make a better world and that begins with knowing ourselves! And we have to use what we got! I see now that change starts from within and ripples out in beautiful ways that I may never know. We are all sharing one planet and humans like me need to start acting like it!"

"How can humans do that, Ms. Girl-illa?" asked Hum, hovering over the crowd.

"Sometimes I think we forget that there are many humans who are making change! Perhaps humanity has the ability to change things for the better. I have asthma but I am learning to breathe easier. I am learning to pause and let my awareness catch up with my monkey mind." Then she put it in practice, closing her eyes and pausing for moment. The words came to here "Let's all take a deep breath together!"

Pacha led the whole stadium to breathe together at once. Still with her eyes closed, her voice cracked a little, "When we breathe together we realize we are single beings on this journey, and at the same time, connected to one another, animated by the same life energy that is in the petal of an orchid, the howl of the wolf, the spirit of Pachamama."

"It's only a few human ideas that are the root of these problems. Now is the time for Pachamama's spirit to sing clearly through humanity. So maybe we can learn to love ourselves, to stop fighting and remember we're actually one earth family! Every day we can bring our favorite instrument to the concert of life!" declared Pacha.

The audience chirped, purred and howled in agreement. Pacha couldn't have been happier! Hum happily chirped:

"I can't wait for the next PACHA JAMMA, so we can grow this seed into a mighty tree with fruit for all. When you all finally make it back home, remember that you are part of a huge burst of positive change that will ripple all around the world."

With that, an eagle and a condor flew together over the stage and into the starry night. Nature sang a song so dazzling that all the children of humanity heard the call in their dreams. All the dreamers were invited to join the party and change the world, and so they did...starting with themselves.

Finally, like all the other children, Pacha woke up in her own bedroom with a giggle. She took a deep breath and felt like the whole world was dancing inside her. Pacha danced joyfully across her bedroom to the mirror, where she joyously discovered that the mushroom on her PJs was winking at her! Something had also changed within her. Pacha was ready to turn her big dreams into an even bigger reality.

Epilogue

For months after her dream adventure, Pacha had gotten along much better with that crazy Mrs. Weezer, mainly because Mrs. Weezer wasn't coming around often. Even when Mrs. Weezer seemed especially determined to visit, Pacha usually figured out ways to completely avoid her by pausing and pacing herself like she did at PACHA JAMMA.

Pacha was counting her blessings - one of her new habits - as she collected trash in the park to make art or science experiments. She had almost filled her entire bag, when she caught a hint of Ms. Weezer. Unsure if it was the truck exhaust or her nervousness about the performance she was to do the next day, Pacha decided to take a breather under the tree in the park where she liked to practice clearing her mind and stretching.

This particular day, pajamas were on her mind. For one, the characters on her pajamas were sleeping later and later. They looked so peaceful sleeping but she was surprised that her mother hadn't noticed. And the other day, Pacha caught a glimpse in the mirror of a Tuba and a Berry scoping out what used to be empty space on the back of her pajama leg. As these thoughts came to her mind, she let them pass like clouds in the sky and refocused on her breath.

Just as she was getting into her breath, several kids passed by, laughing and joking. One of them dropped a plastic hamburger container on the ground in front of Pacha without breaking stride. It was a bully she used to be scared of.

But before she knew what she was doing, Pacha hopped up, and shouted "Hey!" The kids turned and stopped. A boy with the turned-back baseball cap squinted in Pacha's direction saying, "Yeah, what's up?" Pacha recognized the other boys from school too. She wasn't sure what exactly she wanted to say but she knew she had to say something.

She scooted towards the plastic container, saying "I think one of you may have dropped this." Confidently, she scooped up the container, continuing "My name is Pacha. I'm really careful about plastic these days...'cause you never know where it could end up, like a bird's stomach or a whale's blowhole. Have you heard about the ginormous island of plastic in the Pacific Ocean that's bigger than the entire state of Texas?"

The eyes of the boy with the cap lit up. "Whoa! You are Pacha! I had this awesome dream several months ago. There was the huge dance party in nature with plants, animals and kids from everywhere. I was rapping with a platypus, a beatboxing chicken and a hippopotamus... We were talking about being connected as one earth family!"

Pacha grinned and gave him a high ten. "Your dream is my dream too!"

Turning to his friend, Pacha handed the plastic bag to its slightly red-faced owner. "I guess you could throw it away...but where is 'away' anyway? It would be much better to reuse it or turn it into art like I do. Not too mention that hamburgers and other factory-farmed meat are causing so much of this crazy climate chaos around the world!"

She shifted her focus to the entire group. "I did a social experiment last month called the Plastic Challenge, where my family tried to lessen it's plastic waste. It was pretty tough to do, especially for my parents, but these days we're using much less, recycling more and reusing whenever we can. And I just leveled up as a Youth Leader! You could too."

As Pacha started to walk away, she was smiling inside. She felt like she was showing up for the concert of life. Her dreams were encouraging her to do things she hadn't even thought of. Without thinking, she turned back to the kids, saying "By the way, I had a vision of a global dance party that brings us all together! How about we do a flash mob... in our pajamas?"

Fun Facts

That morning, and for the days and nights that followed, Pacha had many more questions for her parents about the animals, plants and all of Nature that had appeared in her dream. Here is just a little bit of what she learned.

Who is Pachamama?

Pachamama is a goddess revered by the indigenous peoples of the South American Andean mountains. Pachamama usually means Mother Earth. In the language of Aymara and Quechua, mama means "mother," and pacha means "world", "land" or "the cosmos." Pachamama and her father, Inti, are some of the most important gods from the Incan Empire, which stretched from present-day Peru through Ecuador and Chile to Argentina. In Incan mythology, Mama Pacha, or Pachamama, is a fertility goddess who watches over planting and harvesting. She can cause earthquakes and great change.

Whale music?

Whales use sound and calling to communicate. The whale belly is a special place for hearing and feeling the music of the oceans. The whale can send a call, or song, around the entire planet's oceans and can connect directly to another whale on the other side of the world! Whales also use sound and calling to "see." This is called echolocation. The sounds bounce off other objects or animals to tell the whale the shape, distance and texture of its surroundings.

Magical hummingbirds?

Hummingbirds can dive at 60 miles per hour—that's as fast as a car driving on the freeway! Their wings beat so quickly that they make a humming sound. To keep up their energy, hummingbirds need to eat every 15 to 20 minutes. They feed off hundreds of flowers per day, drinking their nectar and pollinating the next flower they visit (helping the flowering plants to produce seeds). Hummingbirds are the only birds that can fly backwards, forwards, up, down and sideways, and even float in the air! Legends say the hummingbird is a messenger between worlds, spreading joy, healing and sweetness during times of great change. In many cultures, humming-bird feathers are prized for their magical powers.

What's so awesome about the jaguar?

The jaguar is an important predator that plays a key role in keeping an ecosystem in balance. Quick and agile, the jaguar is the largest of the big cats in the Americas. It is a powerful and beautiful animal found in habitats ranging from desert to rain- forest, but is threatened by hunting and habitat loss. The jaguar is revered in traditional cultures for its spotted coat, and stories have told of its skin magically forming the heavens and stars.

How cool are mushrooms?

Mushrooms were among the first creatures to move onto land from the ocean. They began to live on land 1.3 billion years ago, while plants didn't arrive until 600 million years later. Can you say myco-remediation (my-co-re-mi-di-ay- shun)? It is a process in which mushroom roots, called mycelium, break down and clear contamination of all kinds, like heavy metals, plastics and chemicals, from the environment. By the way, one of the largest living things on the planet is the "honey" mushroom that has been growing in Oregon for 2,400 years and spreads over 2,200 acres. That is the size of 1,665 football fields!

Have you ever heard a tree talking?

Some trees actually "talk" to each other. When a willow tree is attacked by caterpillars or webworms, it lets off a natural chemical that warns other trees nearby of danger. The other trees then start pumping a chemical called tannin into their leaves, making it difficult for insects to swallow the leaves. Trees also can bring on the rain by a process called transpiration—they cool the land by drinking water through their roots and then release that water into the sky through the miniature openings in their leaves. And did you know that one fully grown, leafy tree can provide enough oxygen for 10 people to breathe for a whole year?

How do you relate to your relations?

When the indigenous peoples of the world pray and speak for "All My Relations" (Mitayuke Oyasin in the Lakota language), they are talking not only about our human relatives, but also the spirits of plants, rocks, animals and even natural forces. In fact, all humans are indigenous to somewhere, though some have forgotten their origins. How would your relationship with the world around you be transformed if you saw all things as your mother, father, brother, sister or even yourself? What if you knew that all things that live are supporting one another? This is what Dr. Martin Luther King Jr. meant when he said, "Before you finish eating breakfast this morning, you've depended on more than half the world." In other words, each bite we eat, each item of clothing we wear, each breath we take is a gift from our relations.

What could you do with 8 arms?

All octopi are deaf (but, then again, so was Beethoven)! Octopi actually communicate by changing color, turning white when scared. The average octopus has 1,920 total suction cups on its tentacle arms. When an arm is hurt or cut off, it'll regenerate by re-growing and regenerating the entire arm! The female octopus lays up to 150,000 eggs in two weeks and will poison an enemy by stunning or paralyzing if her babies are threatened.

Can big things come from small pebbles?

Pebbles may be small, but they're hugely important. Pebble tools are some of the earliest known man-made artifacts dating from the Palaeolithic period (hundreds of thousands of years ago). Pebbles show the story of the local geology (rocks) of a place and are actually tiny versions of large mountains.

Got Vitamin N?

It's the vitamin for Nature. Without it, you run the risk of getting Nature Deficit Disorder. That's what it's called when kids don't have access to nature or spend too much time staring at screens. Some of the effects are a lack of attention or being depressed a lot. This is an important reminder to all of us that we need to be close to nature. It's like eating or drinking, but for your spirit. Besides, an ocean or a forest is still the best playground, and a sunset can be better than any TV show!

Does Nature have rights?

Nature's Rights means that species and ecosystems have legal rights to exist, flourish, and naturally evolve. Here are a few new (and old) laws that come from Ecuador and Bolivia:

1) Mother Earth is a living being.
2) Mother Earth is a unique community of beings that sustains all beings.
3) Each being is important because of its relationships.
4) The rights of Mother Earth are basic, like human rights, and are deserved because humans and nature share the same source of existence.

Youth-LeadeR

RECOGNIZED BY UNESCC

WE BRING **INSPIRATION, MEDIA, TOOLS & EMPOWERMENT**
TO OUR GLOBAL GENERATION AT SCHOOL. JOIN US TODAY!

Youth-LeadeR represents **more than 100 young changemakers** evoking extraordinary positive changes in their communities with social entrepreneurship, environmental and humanitarian campaigns.

Our media and methods, applicable by teachers and youth install youth leadership programs in schools, along with services **empowering young people to replicate model solutions**, design their own initiatives, and make changemaking part of daily life.

Julia & Emma
Enormous book drives and eco-literacy programs for ab riginal children and schools

Avalon
Learning about wetlands and restoring amphibian habitats

Robyn
Making water a human right, public, banning bottled water in 27 cities, now scaling nationwide

Join our global community of teachers, student clubs and supporters using exhibits, card games, books, music/al, speaker and webcast services for TAKING ACTION and creating the beautiful future that we all envision for us and generations to come!

Babar
Free teen-powered schools for thousands of poor village kids. Government-accredited, scaling

Gabrielle
Grocers donate, don't dump. 10-fold rise of fre fresh foods for the hung 4,000 volunteers

Xiuhtezcatl
Banning pesticides and fracking mobilizing our generation with Earth Guardian Hip Hop

JOIN US!
USE OUR MEDIA IN 19 LANGUAGES
JOIN THE STUDENT CLUB PROGRAM
ORGANIZE EVENTS & PROGRAMS

bringing unprecedented meaning, purpose, empowerment and **year-round action to thousands of youth**, teachers, families and those impacted around the planet by YL Student Club activities.

Cassandra
Recycling grease to biofuel, donating $100,000 profits to social causes, nov scaling internationally + MANY MO

www.youth-leader.org

EXPLORE OUR INSPIRATIONAL MEDIA, METHODS AND SERVICES ONLINE!

Afterword

When I was a kid, I used to be scared to go to bed because my nightmares were so bad. Yet I remember the first time I dreamt I was a butterfly. I was 7 years old, and I was sleeping on a cot with my mother, who was working as a nurse during the civil war in Nicaragua. Amidst old artillery and trash, I saw myself grow some wings, a golden adventure which carried me above the warzone and into the sunshine song of life. This was one of those healing dreams, where I discovered a newfound appreciation for myself as a hero, someone who could shift perspective on things I had previously been terrified by. It was a moment of metamorphosis, from fear to wonder about myself!

Since then, from India to Jamaica, from stadium stages to all-school assemblies, I have done my best to create opportunities for children and families to overcome their nightmares and discover the dream waiting to come alive. As an entertainer, educator and artist, I believe that we need a change in how we learn and educate, using the power of creativity and imagination to stay "fresh" for the youngest generations.

I feel humbled to have initiated the story of **Pacha's Pajamas**, a story to reflect the ages. The story emerged over a period of 11yrs, from a toddler book to music to the critically-acclaimed brand it is becoming. And it is through such mythic and uplifting stories that the human family might once again awaken to realize our own dreams and our precious connection with all of life.

Pacha's Pajamas emerged as a vision that the child in all of us will awaken to the power of dreams and realize our oneness with Nature, ourselves and the world around us!

Give thanks,

Aaron Ableman